MAVERICKS

SHIPMENT 5

Big Sky Rancher by Carolyn Davidson
The Tracker by Mary Burton
A Convenient Wife by Carolyn Davidson
Whitefeather's Woman by Deborah Hale
Moon Over Montana by Jackie Merritt
Marry Me...Again by Cheryl St.John

SHIPMENT 6

Big Sky Baby by Judy Duarte
The Rancher's Daughter by Jodi O'Donnell
Her Montana Millionaire by Crystal Green
Sweet Talk by Jackie Merritt
Big Sky Cowboy by Jennifer Mikels
Montana Lawman by Allison Leigh
Montana Mavericks Weddings
by Diana Palmer, Susan Mallery

SHIPMENT 7

You Belong to Me by Jennifer Greene
The Marriage Bargain by Victoria Pade
It Happened One Wedding Night by Karen Rose Smith
The Birth Mother by Pamela Toth
A Montana Mavericks Christmas
by Susan Mallery, Karen Rose Smith
Christmas in Whitehorn by Susan Mallery

SHIPMENT 8

In Love with Her Boss by Christie Ridgway
Marked for Marriage by Jackie Merritt
Rich, Rugged...Ruthless by Jennifer Mikels
The Magnificent Seven by Cheryl St.John
Outlaw Marriage by Laurie Paige
Nighthawk's Child by Linda Turner

A FAMILY FOR
THE
HOLIDAYS

VICTORIA PADE

HARLEQUIN® MONTANA MAVERICKS

Special thanks and acknowledgment are given
to Victoria Pade for her contribution to the
MONTANA MAVERICKS: STRIKING IT RICH miniseries.

ISBN-13: 978-0-373-41805-3

Recycling programs
for this product may
not exist in your area.

A Family for the Holidays

Copyright © 2007 by Harlequin Books S.A.

HARLEQUIN®

www.Harlequin.com

Printed in U.S.A.

Victoria Pade is a *USA TODAY* bestselling author of numerous romance novels. She has two beautiful and talented daughters—Cori and Erin—and is a native of Colorado, where she lives and writes. A devoted chocolate lover, she's in search of the perfect chocolate-chip-cookie recipe. For information about her latest and upcoming releases, visit Victoria Pade on Facebook—she would love to hear from you.

Chapter One

Dax Traub's motorcycle sales and repair shop in the heart of Thunder Canyon might as well not have been open on the Monday before Thanksgiving. It was after four o'clock in the afternoon, and not a single person had come through the glass door or so much as paused to peer into the showroom through the storefront windows. He'd spent the day doing exactly what he was doing at that moment—reading articles in motorcycle magazines that were depressing the hell out of him. Articles that—once upon a time—had been about him. Articles that could have been about him *now,* had things turned out differently.

"Scooz me."

The radio was on in the background, and at first Dax thought the small, quiet voice had come from there. But then he realized that a song was playing and that didn't seem likely.

Maybe I'm hearing things...

"Scooz me."

No, he was sure he was hearing something. But with the radio louder than the voice he couldn't tell where the voice was coming from.

He was standing at the counter, facing the front of the store, and no one had come in. But even though it didn't make any sense, he leaned far over the counter and peered down just in case he'd missed something.

There was no one there.

"Scooz me!" The small voice became more insistent and slightly louder. Loud enough for him to finally realize it was coming from behind him.

Dax straightened and glanced over his shoulder.

Sure enough, there stood a little girl to go with the small voice.

He pivoted on his heel to face her, dropping his gaze to the height of a motorcycle tire on display just to the right of the doorway that led to the garage portion of the shop in the rear of the building. That's where the child was standing without any sign of timidity, her head of tousled blond curls held high, her crystal-clear blue eyes waiting expectantly for his attention.

"Hi," he said with a note of question in his tone.

"Hi," the bit-of-nothing responded.

"Can I help you?" he asked.

"I wan' one of these big shiny bikes," the child announced, bypassing Dax and rounding the counter to go into his showroom, dragging a large shoulder-strapped purse along with her.

Dax looked beyond the spot the child had abandoned, wondering if someone else—an adult—was going to appear, too.

No one did, and his tiny customer wasn't allowing him time to investigate because she was talking to him, apparently explaining her need for one of his big shiny bikes.

"Jackass says I'm a baby and my bike is jus' a baby bike and his is a big boy bike and I wan' one tha's bigger 'n his 'cuz I'm not a baby. And red."

Dax followed her onto his showroom floor.

"Jackass?" he repeated, knowing he sounded

thick but unsure exactly what this kid was doing here and talking about.

"He's in my school and he lives on my street, too."

"That's somebody's name? Jackass? Or is that just what you call him because he calls you a baby?" Which was an idea that secretly appealed to the ornery side of Dax.

"Tha's his name—Jackass," the barely-bigger-than-a-minute child said as if it should have been obvious.

Still, he persisted skeptically, asking, "That's his name?"

"Jackass. We haves a lot of Jacks at school —there's Jack W. and Jack M. and Jack—"

"S.," Dax said as light finally dawned. "Jack S."

"Jackass," she confirmed.

Dax couldn't recall the last time he'd smiled, let alone laughed, but one snuck up on him then and he couldn't help chuckling. "Of course. And you want a bike that's bigger than his. And red."

"That one," the little girl said decisively, pointing at a Harley-Davidson classic street bike.

"Good choice," he decreed. "And who might I be selling that one to?"

"To me," she said, once more, as if he were dim-witted.

"And who would you be?"

"I wou' be me." Again a statement of the obvious, only now his lack of understanding brought a frown to crinkle her cherubic face with its rosy cheeks, button nose and ruddy-pink lips.

Dax had no experience or knowledge or contact with children, so he had nothing to gauge how old this one might be. But it was beginning to sink in that, despite her self-assurance, she was very young.

"What's your name?" he said more succinctly.

"Kayla Jane Solomon. Wus yur name?"

"My name? My name is Dax."

"Tha's a funny name."

"Funny or not, that's what it is."

"I haves a friend who gots a dog whose name is Max. Like Max, only Dax?"

"Right," he said, stifling a grin.

"Dax," she repeated, trying it out.

"Kayla Jane Solomon," Dax countered. "And how old are you, Kayla Jane Solomon?"

"Free."

Had she not held up three short fingers, he

would have thought she was answering with something other than a number.

"You're three," he said. "You're Kayla Jane Solomon and you're three years old."

"Free and some months," she elaborated. "But I can never memember how many."

"And where exactly did you come from?" Dax asked.

"The shop," she answered simply.

His building shared a connecting passage with the building directly behind it, and in that other building was the Clip 'n Curl beauty salon. Since his back door and the garage door that opened onto the alley were both closed, the Clip 'n Curl had to be *the shop* she was referring to. Although no one had ever come in here that way before.

"Won't someone be looking for you?"

"I need a bike," she reminded him, refusing to be deterred any longer from her goal.

Dax didn't really know what to do with her. He was bored out of his mind, and this tiny tot was more entertainment than he'd had in a while, so he decided to play along. Temporarily, at any rate.

"How are you going to pay for it?" he asked.

Kayla Jane Solomon dragged the purse

nearer to her, unzipped it and produced a lady's wallet from inside. She opened the wallet, took out the paper money and held it up to him. "Is this 'nough?"

Dax shook his head. "Sorry. Bikes this big cost a lot more than that."

Kayla replaced the money in the wallet, the wallet in the purse and then looked up at him again, still undaunted and now flashing him a smile that was riddled with mischief.

"Maybe you could jus' gib me one, then," she suggested sweetly.

And once again, Dax Traub had to laugh in spite of himself.

"I have a minute now, Kayla. Do you still want a cup of hot choc—"

Shandie Solomon came up short when she stepped into the Clip 'n Curl's break room. Barely fifteen minutes earlier she'd left her three-year-old with a snack and Kayla's favorite DVD playing on a portable DVD player at the table where the stylists sat to eat and chat when they didn't have a customer. Only now, Kayla wasn't there.

"Kayla?" Shandie called from the center of the break room. Sometimes, if the precocious little girl heard her mother coming,

Kayla liked to hide behind the old vinyl sofa that also occupied the space and then jump out to surprise Shandie.

But this time, when she looked behind the couch, she found nothing but dust bunnies.

Kayla wasn't under the microwave stand or hiding beside the refrigerator, so Shandie opted to look in the next likeliest place her daughter might be—the bathroom.

"Kayla? Are you in there?" she said after knocking on the closed restroom door in the hallway outside the break room.

"No, she's not in here," came the answer from one of the other stylists.

"Have you seen her?" Shandie asked.

"She was in the break room when I came in here." An answer that didn't help Shandie at all.

"Okay, thanks," she said, heading back to the main area of the salon.

The entire place was in the middle of the remodeling that was part of the reason Shandie had come to Thunder Canyon. Her cousin Judy had asked her to move to Montana and buy into the business. The Clip 'n Curl, Judy had said, needed new life breathed into it or it wouldn't survive in the town's new climate of change and growth.

Because of the construction, everything was in disarray—a manicure/pedicure area was being built, existing stations were crammed with anything that would fit under their sinks to clear other spaces for work, plumbing and electrical changes were being made, and plastic tarps hung from the ceiling to section off the work being done on new stations. It all made for a number of enticing hiding spots for a tiny three-year-old.

"Kayla?" Shandie repeated yet again, scanning the area. "Has anyone seen my daughter?"

The other stylist, who was coloring a customer's hair, said she hadn't, and the customer chimed in to concur.

From behind one of the tarps, the cabinetmaker said, "She's not in here with me."

Concern began a crawl up Shandie's spine. "She didn't leave the shop, did she?"

The stylist at work on the patron's highlights said, "Not from the front. I've been out here since you picked her up from preschool and brought her in with you, and she hasn't been back this way."

"The bell over the door hasn't gone off, either," the customer contributed.

"But I don't know about the alley door," the stylist added. "Maybe you should check it."

Shandie spun around and picked up her pace, hurrying from there through every possible nook and cranny, even glancing through the window that looked out onto the alley and the motorcycle shop on the opposite side of it. But there were no signs of her daughter.

"She has to be around somewhere," Shandie muttered to herself. Then, in a louder, firmer voice, she said, "Kayla Jane Solomon, where are you?"

Using her daughter's full name should have let the child know she meant business, but still there was no response.

Adrenaline was tying Shandie into tighter and tighter knots.

"Kayla, this isn't funny. Where are you?" she said, feeling and sounding on the verge of terror as her mind raced with awful thoughts.

But again there was no response to her plea.

There were a lot of hiding places in the laundry room, though. In the revamping of the shop Shandie and her cousin were adding massage rooms, a sauna, a relaxation space and a room that would alternate between an aerobic workout room and a yoga room. As a result, the laundry room was now also used for storage, and because Shandie had yet to organize it, things were stacked and piled everywhere.

"Come out now, Kayla," Shandie ordered as she searched behind everything. But this time what Shandie's search brought her to was the door to the utility room. And it was ajar.

"Kayla?" she called again as she opened the door and went in herself.

The buildings that housed the Clip 'n Curl and the motorcycle shop behind it had once been owned by the same person. That person had connected the two properties across the alley, extending the room that contained the Clip 'n Curl's furnace, water heater and electrical panel to reach that other structure. Kayla wasn't in the utility room, either, but there was a door on the other end of it that led to the motorcycle shop. And that door was wide open.

With her heart in her throat once more at the thought of her little girl going through the motorcycle shop and out that front door to who knew where, Shandie crossed the utility closet and rapped on the door that was open into a garage.

"Hello? Anyone?" she called as she went from the utility room into the garage without waiting for an answer or an invitation, too worried about where Kayla might have gone now to hesitate. "Is anybody here? Kayla?"

"We're in front," came a man's voice.

Shandie held her breath, hoping that the *we* included her daughter as she headed across the garage to a doorway that provided access to the sales section of the motorcycle shop. Only when she spotted Kayla did she breathe again, nearly wilting with relief.

"Kayla Jane Solomon, you scared me to death! What are you doing here?" Shandie demanded, rushing to her three-year-old, her focus so concentrated on the child that she was only peripherally aware of the man she knew owned the shop—the somewhat notorious Dax Traub.

"I need a big bike," Kayla informed her simply.

"Apparently Jack S. is giving her a hard time about the size of the bike she has now," her daughter's companion contributed, despite the fact that Shandie continued to stare fiercely at her daughter.

Still, she used his comment as the springboard to say, "And you want to go from a tricycle to a motorcycle?"

"I need a big bike," the little girl repeated.

Shandie closed her eyes, shook her head and sighed, just glad she'd found Kayla and that nothing horrible had befallen her.

Then she opened her eyes, scooped the tiny tot into her arms to hang on to her and finally settled her gaze on the man standing only a few feet away.

"I'm sorry about this," she apologized.

He shrugged it off—literally, with shoulders that were wide and straight and powerful enough to imply, *"Don't mess with me."*

"No problem," he said. "I do sell big bikes, after all. It was the logical place to come for one."

Shandie appreciated that he was making light of it. "I'm sure you didn't need a three-year-old wasting your time, though."

"Actually, she's been my only customer today. Wasting time is all I've done, and she was a nice change of pace."

A smile went with that information. Not a huge grin, merely a minor upturning of the corners of a mouth that was a touch on the full side.

"I guess it's good she didn't blow your biggest sale or something, then," Shandie said.

Belatedly she realized she hadn't introduced herself, and so she added, "I'm Shandie Solomon, by the way."

"Dax Traub."

"Like Max the dog, only Dax," Kayla explained.

Shandie didn't tell either of them that she knew who Dax Traub was. Besides the fact that she'd seen him a time or two coming and going from the rear of his store, and he was too attractive a man not to notice, his name had cropped up on occasion among some of the women who frequented the Clip 'n Curl. Enough so that Shandie was aware that Dax Traub was the dauntingly good-looking daredevil, hell-raiser, heartbreaker and all-round bad boy who currently had tongues wagging about a very sudden—and very brief—engagement to someone, a rift with his brother over someone else he'd formerly been married to, as well as apparently uncharacteristically dour spirits that had turned him dark and brooding and had him avoiding old friends who were all wondering what was going on with him.

Although at that moment Shandie didn't

see anything that seemed dark or brooding about his mood since he appeared to be amused by her daughter's misbehavior.

"I'm Judy Johnson's cousin," Shandie said then. "She sold me a half interest in the Clip 'n Curl, and we're in the process of expanding and remodeling. Judy had to leave town— her mother had some health problems and Judy has to stay with her until her mother is back on her feet. So I'm overseeing everything along with trying to build my own client base, and Kayla was supposed to be having an after-school snack and watching the Wiggles in the break room."

"Seems more like she *had* the wiggles," Dax Traub joked.

"Anyhow, there's a lot of work going on in the utility room because we need to add a second water heater and another electrical box, and that must have been how Kayla discovered the room and found her way through to you." Shandie wasn't sure why she was giving the man such a lengthy explanation. Although it did provide the opportunity to look at him a while longer, and she was enjoying that. Even if it did make her feel slightly jittery inside.

"I need a big bike," Kayla said yet again as

if that was the reason she'd ended up where she had despite what her mother was postulating.

"These are motorcycles, not bicycles, and they aren't for little girls," Shandie informed her daughter.

"I'm a *big* girl," Kayla insisted.

"Not motorcycle-big, you aren't," Shandie countered.

Ignoring the mother-daughter debate, Dax Traub commented instead on what Shandie had said about the Clip 'n Curl. "I know there's been a lot going on back there for a while now. I heard all the noise and wondered what was up."

"It wasn't supposed to take this long, but I guess that's how construction goes. We started in the summer and here it is—Thanksgiving on Thursday—and we're still further away from being finished than I even want to think about."

"I've had a lot on my mind lately, but are you saying that you've been around since the summer—right behind me—and I've missed it?"

"I haven't actually been around much until the last few weeks. Judy and I worked up the plans for what we wanted to do while she was visiting me in Denver, and she got it started. I've been in and out of Thunder Canyon to deal with a few things on the shop and to find a place to live, but I had a house that had to be sold and a whole life to wrap up in Colorado before I could make the move."

Dax Traub nodded as if that accounted for why he hadn't known she existed before. He also suddenly seemed to be making up for lost time by studying her, and Shandie became very self-conscious under the scrutiny. She couldn't help taking mental stock of her unimpressive jeans and the equally unimpressive tennis shoes she'd worn today for comfort. And the black smock all the stylists used to protect their clothing totally hid the fact that she had on a T-shirt she considered one of her better ones because it was formfitting and gave the illusion that she was a C-cup rather than barely a B.

At least she knew her shoulder-length blond hair was in good shape because she'd had one of the other girls highlight it just that morning. She'd also done her blush, mascara and lipstick right before leaving the shop to pick up Kayla from preschool, so while she might be wearing something tantamount to a choir robe, her high cheekbones, blue eyes and not-too-full, not-too-thin lips were taken care of, enough to leave her presentable.

Still, she felt at a disadvantage, and just as she was about to end this encounter to escape, it registered that her purse was on the floor near where Kayla had been standing.

"You took my purse?" she asked her daughter, retrieving it to sling over her shoulder.

"She was going to pay for the bike with what's inside," Dax Traub said, again seeming to find some humor in the situation.

"Kayla! You know better than that!"

"You don't gots 'nough money. But we could use the bad charge 'cuz this is a 'mergency."

Embarrassed by that, Shandie grimaced and felt obliged to explain again. "That sounds worse than it is. The *bad* charge is bad because it's the account I have a balance on and am trying to pay off. I only use it in emergencies." Then, to her daughter, she said, "And you getting a motorcycle isn't an emergency."

"I *need* a big bike," Kayla said in a tone that Shandie knew could elevate into a tantrum.

She had no idea if Dax Traub was aware of that, too, but before Kayla could take it that far he changed the subject. "So how do you both like old Thunder Canyon?" he asked.

Her earlier thought of ending this encounter drifted away with the opportunity to go on talking to him and Shandie said, "I like it a lot. Or what I've seen of it. I haven't really been able to pay attention to more than the necessities yet, and even though a fair share of people come through the shop, I haven't made any friends or anything, but I'm sure that will come."

He nodded a head that was so smolderingly handsome it could have graced one of the posters for men's hairstyles that came to the shop on a monthly basis. And he had hair great enough to qualify as a poster boy, too. Thick, shiny deep mink-colored hair, cut short on the sides and in the back, and left longer on top in finger-combed waves, that had a charm—and a sexiness—all its own.

He also had eyes that were so dark brown they were the color of espresso beans, bordered by lashes so thick they should have been outlawed. His nose was slightly hawkish above those supple lips, and his facial structure included pronounced cheekbones and a jawline that could have been carved from granite. Plus, he was tall, lean and muscular, and couldn't have been better suited to the low-slung jeans he was wearing with a gray sweatshirt over a white T-shirt, under a denim jacket, with the sweatshirt's hood pulled above the jacket's collar in back.

"I'd better get going," Shandie said when she realized silence had fallen between them and she was the one doing the staring now and really should end this whole thing. "I have a haircut due in any minute."

"I still need a big bike," Kayla reminded her.

"She's three," Shandie said. "I think there's a handbook somewhere that says she gets points for persistence."

Dax Traub smiled again and aimed his dark eyes at Kayla. "You tell Jack S. that you know where there are a lot of bikes bigger than his and if he doesn't leave you alone I'll bring one over to show him what a baby *he* is."

Shandie flinched. "Oh, don't say that. She'll make you stick to it."

"That's okay. We have to keep these hot-shots in line," he said.

"I'll tell 'im," Kayla assured, clearly feeling victorious.

"Anyway, again, I'm sorry for bothering you," Shandie said before any more promises could be made.

Dax Traub's smile this time was pure devilish charisma, and he flashed it at mother and daughter. "No bother. I'm glad I got to meet you. Both."

"Nice to meet you, too," Shandie said, not sounding anywhere near as smooth as he did. "Do you mind if I go out the way I came in?" she added with a nod toward the garage.

"I can't think of a reason I would."

"Okay, thanks. And thanks for not letting Kayla get any farther away than your showroom."

"Sure."

"Bye, Dax-like-Max-the-dog," Kayla said, being silly and swiveling on her mother's hip so she could look over Shandie's shoulder at the shop owner as Shandie turned to go.

"Bye, Kayla Jane Solomon," he countered as if they were sharing a private joke.

Which they must have been because her daughter giggled.

"Feel free to come and see me again," he added.

Shandie wasn't sure if he was talking to her or to Kayla or to them both and as she reached the doorway to the garage she glanced over her own shoulder to see if she could tell.

But all she saw was Dax Traub smiling

again, crookedly, and with enough mischief to leave more questions than answers.

And to confirm what she'd garnered from the things she'd heard said about him even before she'd met him—that Dax Traub was trouble.

Fun trouble.

But definitely trouble.

Which was the last thing Shandie Solomon was looking for.

Chapter Two

Tuesday was unbelievably busy for Shandie. The days before any holiday were usually booked solid with people wanting to look their best for upcoming celebrations, and even without an established client list she had back-to-back appointments scheduled. She also ended up dealing with a disgruntled plumber, construction havoc, an electrician who wanted to cut off all the power rather than only a section of the shop at a time, and two trips to the bakery to replenish the goodies she was using as incentive to keep customers coming in during the remodeling.

Along with getting Kayla to and from preschool and making sure her daughter was taken care of once Kayla was at the shop afterward, it certainly seemed to Shandie that that should have been more than enough to keep her mind occupied. And yet thoughts of Dax Traub had still managed to creep through the cracks when she least expected them.

It was a problem she'd had since she'd met him the previous day. The whole way home, the entire evening with Kayla, as Shandie had tried reading in bed the night before, Dax Traub had intruded.

He'd been on her mind the moment her alarm had snatched her from sleep this morning, too. He'd plagued her thoughts all through getting herself and her daughter ready for the day. But she'd been convinced that getting to work, pouring herself into her job, would finally put an end to it.

Only it hadn't. And as she escorted the last customer out of the shop, told Kayla to pick up her toys and headed for the laundry room to fold clean towels for Wednesday, Shandie was frustrated with herself.

Of course, she might have had better luck *not* thinking about Dax Traub today at work if the subject of him hadn't come up again and again throughout the day, she thought.

Women customers she didn't know and who would otherwise not have drawn her notice had made her all-ears at the repeated mention of his name.

Not that the conversations about him had been particularly enlightening. They'd been basically speculation and curiosity about whether or not he would go to the big pre-Thanksgiving dinner his friends were having Wednesday evening at The Rib Shack, the new restaurant Dax's brother, D.J., had just returned to Thunder Canyon to open at the ski resort. There was particular concern about a recent fistfight between the brothers and whether it might be repeated if Dax *did* go.

There was also concern about Dax himself. Apparently, none of his old friends knew what was up with him lately or how to bring him out of his funk, or whether it was better to leave him to sort through his problems on his own, whatever those problems were—and no one was completely clear about that, either.

There was something *she* was perfectly clear about, however, Shandie thought as she stood at the dryer folding towels. When she added the information she'd gathered about Dax Traub—vague though it was—to the other things she'd heard through the grapevine, she knew it was that much more ridiculous for her to be giving the man a second thought.

So why had the image of him, the memory of the sound of his voice and every word he'd said, followed her through the past twenty-four hours like a stubborn ghost determined to haunt her? Why had she seized every opportunity to come into this laundry room and peer out the window at the alley and the rear of the motorcycle shop?

And, each time she had, why had she felt a hint of hope that she would catch a glimpse of the man himself, and then been let down when she hadn't?

It doesn't matter why, she told herself as she suffered the gazillionth wave of that disappointment when—in the course of folding the towels—she'd just gone through the whole process once again. It didn't matter *why* she'd been so distracted by thoughts of Dax Traub or that she'd been peeking out at his shop to catch sight of him—it just needed to stop.

"So stop it," she ordered under her breath even as her gaze drifted through the glass to the rear of his place.

She wanted to. She honestly did. Thunder Canyon was a fresh start for her. Leaving

Denver and all the reminders of Pete was a big step, and she'd finally been able to take it because she was ready to move on. The past three and a half years had been rough, but she'd made her way through it all and she honestly felt as if she'd come out on the other side of a mountain. She'd even talked to Judy about maybe dating once she got to Thunder Canyon.

But *maybe* dating—down the road, at some point—some ordinary nice guy who Judy might possibly set her up with or who she might meet here, was different than being consumed with thoughts of a guy she'd only exchanged a few words with. A guy who—although he was hellaciously handsome—was clearly complicated. Who apparently didn't have a good relationship with his own family. A guy who might have a chip on his shoulder and who—at the very least—obviously didn't have much staying power when it came to women if he already had a divorce under his belt and had impulsively become engaged and then unengaged to someone.

That was not just some nice, ordinary guy she might possibly, under the right circumstances, consider going to dinner with or seeing a movie with as her first dip-of-the-toe into the dating pool again. *That* was a guy to stay far, far away from. For her own sake and for Kayla's.

Especially for Kayla's sake, she told herself firmly.

She absolutely would not put her daughter in the vicinity of anyone Kayla might come to care about or depend on, only to have that person turn his back on them.

No, Pete was a hard act to follow. He'd been a genuinely, thoroughly good man. A trustworthy, caring, unselfish, dependable, feet-on-the-ground man. A man she and Kayla could have counted on forever, had fate not intervened.

A man who couldn't easily be replaced and would have to be lived up to if ever anyone was in the running to replace him.

And not only was Dax Traub not in the running to replace Pete—nor was there any evidence that he wanted to be—but even if he was, Dax Traub was about the most unlikely man to ever take the place of Pete Solomon.

So, she really did need to stop thinking about Dax Traub. And picturing him and his dark, deep eyes and how she'd felt as if they could heat the surface of her skin when they were aimed at her, and how sexy he was when he smiled.

No, Dax Traub was just someone nice to look at. But only from a long way away. Like lions at the zoo. He was a sight to see, to gaze upon, to appreciate the glory of from a distance. But only trained lion tamers should get in the cage with him.

"And that isn't me," Shandie muttered as she folded the towels.

She was just the mother of a three-year-old who was going to put the towels away once they were folded and take Kayla home for dinner and a quiet evening. Just the two of them. Safe and sound and secure and comfortable.

Far outside the lion's den.

"I wan' a peanut butter and marsh'allow sam'ich for dinner."

Shandie would have taken issue with her daughter's announcement as she applied the car key to the ignition, but when the engine didn't start that became the priority.

"Just a minute," she told her daughter, postponing the conversation as she tried again.

But again nothing happened.

"Uh-oh," she said. "Something's wrong with the car."

"Turn it on," Kayla suggested logically.

"I'm trying," Shandie said as she did just that, making four more attempts. All with no result. "Great."

For the first time since Dax Traub had been popping into her head for no reason, Shandie welcomed the intrusion. Because it suddenly occurred to her that the man owned and operated his own motorcycle shop. That he repaired the things. And if he could make *them* run, maybe he could make her car run, too.

If he hadn't closed up for the day and gone home already.

She quickly got out from behind the wheel of her sedan, took Kayla from the car seat in the back and carried the little girl for a fast return trip to the Clip 'n Curl.

"You said we wuz goin' home," Kayla complained. "And I wan' peanut butter and marsh'allow—"

"The car is broken, and we need some help."

Kayla accepted that without further comment, and Shandie wasted no time rushing with her daughter through the dark beauty shop, through the laundry room to the utility space behind it.

The door that connected the motorcycle shop's garage was closed but—gratefully—not locked. Much as she had the day before, Shandie knocked and went through to the garage without waiting for a response.

"Hello? Are you still here?" she called.

Dax Traub appeared at the doorway that connected the showroom, pulling a black leather aviator jacket on over a Henley sweater and jeans. "You lookin' for me?" he asked.

Too many times today, Shandie thought.

But what she said was, "I'm so glad I caught you. My car won't start. I know motorcycles are your thing, but I thought maybe—"

"What's it doing?"

"Hi!" Kayla said belatedly, brightly and as if she were thrilled to have this second encounter with the man.

Dax Traub paused to aim a just-as-thrilled-to-see-her smile at the child, winked at her and answered her greeting with a warm, "Hey, Kayla Jane Solomon."

"Hey, Dax-like-Max-the-dog," Kayla responded then, giggling with delight.

"The car's not doing anything," Shandie

said when the two of them were finished with their playful exchange. "When I turn the key there's a little clicking noise and that's it."

"How old is your battery?"

Shandie shrugged. "As old as the car—seven years."

"That's probably the problem. Are you parked somewhere I can get to it to give you a jump?"

Shandie hadn't thought of the battery. "No, I'm nose-first in that little space on the side of the shop that's big enough for only one car."

He nodded. "I know that spot. But I'll tell you what—the temperature's dropping, it's dark, and it'll be tough to get to the battery at all in that cubbyhole of a parking place. So how about if I give you two a ride home, and tomorrow when it's warmer and we have some daylight, I'll take a look? Chances are I'll be able to hook up your battery to my charger and that'll take care of it. Otherwise, we're going to have to tow you out of there and that's more complicated and also something better done when I can see."

Jump her...

Hook up his charger to her battery...

He hadn't said any of that with any sort of

undertone or innuendo, and yet sexy under-tones and innuendos were flitting through her brain anyway.

Such thoughts were hardly typical of her, and she didn't know why it was happening to her now.

"I'm sure it's just the battery," she muttered to conceal what was going through her head. Then, forcing herself to focus on more mun-dane matters, she said, "I'll have to get back here tomorrow, but I guess I can ask one of the other girls to bring me in."

"Can we ride home on a big bike?" Kayla asked, excited by the idea.

Shandie hadn't considered that possibility, and before Dax had answered her daughter she said, "Are you taking us home on the back of a motorcycle?"

He laughed wryly at her alarm. "No, I own a truck, too." He nodded toward the utility room door behind her then. "Do you have to go back?"

"No, everything is locked up and turned off. This is the only unlocked door," she said, poking a thumb over her shoulder at the panel she'd come through.

"That lock was broken when I set up here. I've never fixed it."

"You probably should. It would keep little girls out," Shandie said.

"Yeah, but the problem with that is that it would keep big girls out, too," he countered pointedly and with the kind of smooth, easy-to-come-by charm Shandie was sure had earned him his bad-boy reputation.

She pretended not to catch the flirtatious undertone even as something tingly erupted just beneath the surface of her skin. "I do need Kayla's car seat out of my car," she said. "I could go get it and bring it over here or you could pull your truck around and meet us—"

"Why don't I just drive us all around the block? Kayla'll be okay riding in your lap that long, won't she?"

"Sure," Shandie agreed.

"Le's go!" Kayla said, apparently equally as excited by the idea of riding in Dax's truck as she had been by the thought of riding one of his motorcycles.

"You're the boss," Dax decreed, leading the way through his showroom, locking his own shop after them and pointing out his truck parked in front.

It was a black behemoth big enough to cart two motorcycles in the bed and to haul a trailer with four more if need be, he explained as they got in and went the short distance to Shandie's car.

Once they arrived there, Shandie left Kayla with Dax and got the safety seat, but when she returned with it to the truck, Dax was waiting on the passenger side to put it in for her.

Shandie appreciated the courtesy, but he didn't know what he was doing and after a few failed attempts to figure it out she took over. As she did he went around to stand by while Kayla stood behind the truck's steering wheel, bouncing wildly in her mimicry of driving.

Shandie had to smile to herself when he began to teach her daughter to make engine noises, but she didn't comment on how funny it sounded.

Then the car seat was strapped in tightly to the center of the truck's bench seat.

"Okay, climb in," Shandie told the little girl.

After some reluctance to leave the wheel, Kayla did get into the carrier, wiggling until her heavy quilted coat wasn't bunched up around her, then settling and promptly taking off her knitted hat and mittens.

It was something she inevitably did the

minute Shandie got her in the car seat, and Shandie had given up fighting to stop it because she never won anyway—as soon as she wasn't looking, off went hat and gloves every time.

As Shandie buckled her daughter in, Dax got behind the wheel once more. "Where to?" he asked.

Shandie recited her address in the course of situating herself again in the passenger seat and closing the side door so they could get going once more.

"Huh?"

"It isn't far," she said as if his *huh* had indicated that he thought it was.

"No, I know."

"Is it a bad neighborhood or something?"

"I live on the same street—so maybe," he joked.

"Which house?" Shandie asked, surprised to learn they lived near each other.

"The big gray one on the corner closest to New Town."

"That *is* a big house. But I thought a family lived there with a teenager."

"I rent out the main floor and live in the apartment on the second level. The income from the renters helps tide things over during the slow winter months. What house are you in?"

"The small yellow one, second from the other end."

"So we've been within walking distance of each other there, too? I really must have been in a fog lately."

"Well, at least you won't have to go far out of your way," Shandie said.

"Wouldn't have mattered if I had needed to," he assured her with a sideways glance that seemed along the same lines as his comment about not fixing the lock on the utility room door and blocking big girls from coming into his garage.

Shandie didn't know what to say except, "Well, I appreciate the lift," and only after she'd said it did she realize he was giving a bit of a lift to her ego, too, since she was feeling flattered to be flirted with for the first time in a very long while.

Kayla caught her attention then. Sitting in her carrier between them, out of the blue the toddler began to rub the sleeve of Dax Traub's leather jacket.

It *did* look as soft as butter, and Shandie was aware of a curiosity of her own about whether or not it felt the way it looked. But being three and having few inhibitions, Kayla merely reached over and rubbed Dax's arm.

It took him by surprise and he glanced from the road to the chubby hand caressing his coat.

"Kayla..." Shandie reprimanded.

"Feels like blankie," the little girl countered.

"It isn't blankie, though, so keep your hands to yourself," Shandie said, embarrassed.

Or was it not *only* embarrassment she was feeling? Was there also some envy over the fact that her daughter was getting to touch Dax Traub?

It had better just be embarrassment, she told herself.

"It's okay," he assured Shandie as Kayla went right on fingering the leather the way she did the satin edge of her favorite blanket when she was falling asleep.

"Ever'body was talkin' 'bout you today," the little girl said then.

Dax aimed another look at Shandie, and she could tell he was taking her daughter's remark to mean that Shandie had been talking about him today.

"Not me," she was quick to say. Too quick. "But you *were* the talk of the beauty shop."

Although she hadn't thought that Kayla had been eavesdropping as much as she had been.

One of Dax's eyebrows arched suspiciously. "Why?"

"A few of the customers knew each other and were wondering if you'll go to some dinner they're having tomorrow night?" She finished that in the form of a question because it wasn't as if she was clear about what she was referring to.

Dax turned his eyes to the road ahead, and as Shandie looked over at his perfect profile she saw his chin raise slightly in what might have been defensiveness or defiance or maybe both—she couldn't tell. But it had a stiffness to it that let her know she'd hit a sore spot.

"It's none of my business," she said in a hurry to provide an excuse for him not to talk about it.

"It's okay," he said. Then, when Shandie expected him to drop it, he added, "Some old friends are having a get-together is all."

"A pre-Thanksgiving dinner," Shandie repeated what she'd overheard.

"Right."

"And you may not go?" she asked cautiously.

"It's pretty unlikely, yeah," he said in a

gruff voice that was almost more to himself than to her.

"It sounded nice," she offered. "Good food. Everyone's looking forward to it..."

"Probably more if they can count on my not being there."

"I didn't get that impression."

"No? What impression did you get?"

Shandie shrugged within the navy-blue peacoat she had buttoned to her throat. "I got the impression that they wanted you to go."

He gave her a look that said he doubted that.

"Why would they invite you and *not* want you to be there? Especially if they're old friends?"

"Because now one of the old friends is coupled with my ex-fiancée, and my ex-wife has connected with my brother, who's not so thrilled with me himself and... It's complicated."

"Oh," Shandie said, not telling him that she'd heard he'd had a fight with his brother. After all, she didn't actually know anything about it, anyway. Or any details about any of the rest of what he'd just briefly outlined.

"Still," she felt inclined to persist, "I didn't

get the idea that anyone wanted you to miss the dinner."

"Yeah, well, I can't say I'm too thrilled about going myself."

"Oh. Is this a group you want out of?" she asked, treading carefully.

He shot her a quizzical look, as if he didn't know why she'd ask that.

"It happens," she said in defense of her question. "People reach points in friendships and even in families where they just don't want to be a part of it anymore."

"I thought we were only talking about some dumb dinner?"

And clearly he didn't welcome her sticking her nose into any more than that.

Shandie took the hint and shrugged. "All I know is that if I were you, I'd go."

"Why?"

"It's Thanksgiving, the start of the holiday season, your friends are getting together, it sounds fun, and I say bury whatever hatchets there are. Go, have a good time, forget about anything else that's gone on."

They'd reached their common street and her house. Dax pulled into her driveway. He put the engine into Park and applied the emergency brake but left the engine and the heater on as he slung one wrist over the top of the steering wheel and pivoted enough to look her eye-to-intense-espresso-brown-eye.

Shandie might have thought he was angry except that around his lips was just the teaser of a mischief-filled smile.

"I'll go if you will," he said offhandedly.

"Me?" Shandie exclaimed. "Where did that come from? I wasn't invited."

"Maybe I'm inviting you. I can bring someone, why not you? At least then I'd know that one of us would benefit from it."

"Why *not* me? Because whoever is going to be there doesn't know me and I don't know them—even the women who were talking about you today weren't my clients and—"

"That's how you *get* to know people—you go somewhere, get introduced, spend some time with them."

"And I have Kayla and—"

"That teenager whose family I rent to? She's fifteen and she babysits for people in the neighborhood all the time. She'd probably be happy to stay with Kayla, and Kayla would love her. Wouldn't you, Kayla?"

"Can she make peanut butter and marsh'allow sam'iches?" the three-year-old asked.

"Probably," Dax said.

"Okay."

"Besides," he said to Shandie again, "you said yesterday that you haven't met anyone you'd consider a friend yet. This would give you the chance to get out and do that. To socialize."

"I just think *you* should go," she contended. "That you might be sorry if you don't. Besides, I wasn't looking to get myself in on it." Although it did appeal to her.

"I didn't think you were," Dax assured. "Even though it does seem to have lit a spark in you."

"I wouldn't say that," Shandie lied.

She wasn't positive, but she thought he was teasing her. Toying with her to amuse himself—again like a true bad boy showing his ornery streak. But the more she thought about being included in the next night's get-together, the more inclined she was to call what she thought might be his bluff and agree to go.

Even if she did, though, she wasn't going to let him turn this into something he did for her sake. "I think if you *don't* go it could give a negative message that might end up with people reading more into it than you want them to. That is, if you genuinely aren't looking to get out of this group. So, unless you want to cause problems and questions about why you wouldn't have dinner with your old friends and your brother, you *should* go."

"Is that right?"

"That's what I think," she said.

"With nothing to base it on but some beauty shop gossip?"

"With nothing to base it on but my own intuition and the sense I got from what little I overheard today. Your friends are wondering what's going on with you, and if you don't show up tomorrow night, they'll be wondering even more."

"How about you?" he asked with a sly twinkle in his eyes. "Are you wondering what's going on with me?"

"It's none of my business," she repeated as if her curiosity about him wasn't growing by the minute.

Still he wasn't forthcoming. He merely smiled more broadly. "Maybe you'll find out if you come to that dinner with me."

"Would you feel better about it if you didn't have to go alone?"

He grinned. "Would you feel better about

going if I say I'd feel better about going if I didn't have to go alone?"

Shandie was beginning to think this was a game she wasn't any more likely to win than the struggle to keep Kayla's hat and mittens on in the car seat. So she conceded.

"Yes," she said. "It does sound like fun, and it would give me a chance to meet some people. I think it would be good for you to go, and so if it would make you more comfortable, I'd be happy to go with you. As long as it was just as friends and as your moral support, to pay you back for taking us home tonight and fixing my car tomorrow."

His grin got even wider as he volleyed once more in the game she'd been trying to put an end to. "If that makes *you* feel better—just as friends, payback for the ride and for the jump tomorrow, no strings attached."

Shandie took a deep breath and sighed. "Okay."

He laughed as if he'd thoroughly enjoyed whatever it was they'd just played. "Gee, thanks," he said facetiously.

Shandie rolled her eyes at him and released the portion of Kayla's car seat that kept the little girl contained. Then she got out of the truck and turned back to help Kayla climb from the carrier. The three-year-old jumped across that section of seat into Shandie's arms so Shandie could lift her down to the ground.

While she did, Dax unclicked the belt that held the safety seat and took it with him to cart up to the front door behind Shandie and Kayla.

"Can Dax-like-Max-the-dog have sam'iches with us?" Kayla asked as they made the trek.

"You aren't having peanut butter and marshmallow sandwiches for dinner, Kayla, no matter what," Shandie said, recognizing her daughter's tactics and uncomfortable with the spot the child's question put her in. But after already considering asking Dax to stay, she'd thought better of it.

"But I *wan'* peanut butter and marsh'allow sam'iches!" Kayla insisted.

Shandie unlocked the door. "Go in and take off your coat," she said, rather than getting sucked into what she knew was likely to be a battle.

"*Then* can I have 'em?" Kayla bargained.

"Maybe you can have marshmallows in hot chocolate before bed if you eat a good—not sweet—dinner," Shandie countered to avoid the fight.

That appeased her daughter, who paused to say "Bye" to Dax before going inside.

Alone on the porch with Dax, Shandie turned and took the car seat from him. "Thanks," she said, echoing the word but not the facetious tone he'd used moments earlier.

"Sure," he answered. "Want me to send Misty down to meet you?"

"Misty?"

"The babysitter," he said with a nod in the direction of his house up the street.

"It's cold and a school night. I'd hate to make her come out. Maybe you could just give me her number and I'll call her?" Shandie suggested, taking a pen and one of her business cards out of her purse.

She handed them both to him, and Dax wrote on the back of the card in the space allotted for appointment dates and times. Then he returned it to her.

"I put my numbers on there, too. In case you want to back out of tomorrow night for some reason," he said, letting her know he wouldn't hold her to something he'd essentially taunted her into in the first place.

Shandie couldn't think of any reason she'd want to back out, but she didn't tell him that.

Instead she said, "I'll see you in the morning, then? With your battery charger?"

"First thing," he promised before he said goodnight and retraced his steps to his still-running truck.

Only in his wake did it strike Shandie that she'd just made what could be considered a date with him.

With Dax Traub.

And that was when a reason to back out of dinner with him the following night did occur to her.

It was a date.

With Dax Traub....

Chapter Three

What *was* going on with him?

It was the question that Shandie had said people were throwing around the beauty shop, and as Dax got ready for Wednesday night's dinner, it was something he was wondering himself. Again—because the truth was, it was something he'd been wondering for a while now.

He'd turned thirty this year, and it had hit him hard. It was an age, he thought as he got into the shower, when there was no more denying he was an adult, that his life had gotten to where it was going. And he'd had to take stock.

His friends, the guys he'd grown up with

and known all his life—Grant Clifton, Marshall and Mitchell Cates, Russ Chilton and even his own brother, D.J.—were all around the same age. And yet if they looked back, they could all list success in their lives, their careers and in their relationships—since most of them had found women they wanted to spend their futures with. And where was he?

Nowhere.

Business was lousy. His marriage had lasted only a few years. That flash-in-the-pan engagement to Lizbeth Stanton...

What *was* going on with him? he asked himself.

He wished he knew.

Maybe a better question was what the hell had happened to him.

He'd been on top of the world all through high school. He'd thought he was cool, and so had everyone else. Girls had fallen all over him, there had never been a party he wasn't invited to, a person who hadn't wanted to hang out with him. He'd snatched Thunder Canyon's golden girl from under every other guy's nose—apparently including his brother's, even though he hadn't known how D.J. had felt about Allaire at the time. And fresh from graduation and his honeymoon, he'd begun what had proved to be one of the most stupendous winning streaks motorcycle racing had ever seen.

He'd had it all, and he'd been sure that his entire future would be the stuff of dreams....

Shampoo suds were running down his face. He clamped his eyes shut, stepped under the spray of the shower and let the water beat down on him.

The stuff of dreams...

Then his fresh-out-of-high-school marriage to Allaire had tanked.

And fast on the heels of that, his biggest dream had ended in a nightmare against a retaining wall.

And when all the dust had settled and the stitches had come out and the casts and bandages had been removed, he'd found himself with no choice but to try picking up what pieces he could salvage from what was left.

That was where the shop had begun.

But it wasn't booming, and he knew why. Sure, he was good with an engine, with the mechanics, working with his hands, but his heart just wasn't in the business that seemed like nothing more than a consolation prize.

So here he was, a washout at thirty. A loser.

Or at least that was what he felt like. A royally messed-up, couldn't-make-anything-work-out, didn't-know-what-he-wanted loser. Who probably deserved the strained way all his friends were acting around him and the fight he'd had with his brother.

Maybe he should lock up, load his Harley into the back of the truck and get the hell out of Thunder Canyon, he thought as he went on standing in the punishing spray of the shower. Maybe he should go somewhere where he could forget everything here—past and present—and start over.

He considered it. Seriously. Even contemplating where he might go.

But that didn't do anything for him either, he realized. In fact, it seemed like an even more dreary route to take.

Thunder Canyon was still home. Still where he'd grown up. Where he felt he belonged.

"But something's gotta give," he growled.

Going nowhere, enjoying nothing, adrift and wondering, *What now?* It sucked.

Although it struck him suddenly that the *enjoying nothing* part wasn't altogether true of the past few days. He'd enjoyed Kayla Solomon. And Kayla Solomon's mom...

Just the thought of the two of them lifted his spirits a little.

Kayla with her tousled hair and three-year-old's confidence—sure of herself, of what she wanted, of how she could get it.

And her mom.

Shandie Solomon.

He'd heard there was someone new at the Clip 'n Curl who was worth a look. It just hadn't really registered through his misery and he hadn't given it a second thought. Or put any effort into taking a look.

But to say that Shandie was worth a look was an understatement.

Shandie Solomon was hotter than hell.

She and her daughter shared the same hair color—blond so blond it nearly gleamed. They had the same pale skin, too, and Shandie's was no less smooth or flawless than the little girl's. Their eyes tagged them as mother and daughter as well. The blue of a mountain sky on a clear winter's day, and with the longest lashes he'd ever seen.

Shandie also had a small, perfect nose, which was slightly different from her daughter's upturned little pug, and high cheekbones and bone structure that looked fine and delicate, as opposed to Kayla's chubby cheeks.

And then there was Shandie's compact, not-too-thin, not-too-curvy body—he'd wanted to pull that up against him and...

Dax dropped his head backward and shook it as a dog shakes water from its coat, despite the continued pelting of the shower.

The last thing he needed to be thinking about was pulling some woman—any woman—up against him.

He grabbed the bar of soap to get on with his shower. And as he lathered up, he reminded himself that he wasn't interested in starting anything with Shandie Solomon—or anyone else—right now.

After the fiasco with Lizbeth he knew better than to think a woman could be the bandage that would fix his screwed-up life, and he was determined to sort everything out before he let himself get involved with anyone again. He knew that was the only hope he had of getting it right, and he just couldn't take any more failures.

So why was he going to this dinner tonight and taking Shandie Solomon with him?

Another good question.

Maybe because when he was with Kayla and Shandie, he got a rest from his own depressing thoughts. He actually forgot about how damn unhappy he'd been lately.

So when Shandie had started talking about this dinner—which he'd had no intention of going to until she'd brought it up—and he'd heard in her voice how much she would have liked it if she had been included in something like it, the whole thing hadn't seemed like such a bad idea.

Especially when taking her also meant that he was certain to see her again tonight—without having to hope her daughter might sneak into his shop again and act as a lure for her mother to follow, or that the car battery he'd charged today might not hold the charge and give him the chance to take them home again.

But he was probably making a mistake, he told himself as he rinsed off the soap. It was probably a mistake to go to this dinner when he and his brother were liable to fight again. When his ex-wife and ex-fiancée would be there. When everybody was walking on eggshells around him and playing down their own successes and happiness rather than make his lousy life seem even worse.

Going to this dinner was probably a mistake when spending an entire evening with Shandie Solomon would give free rein to a weakness for her that he shouldn't be having at all, let alone giving in to. Particularly since it would undoubtedly just feed the thoughts and mental images he'd been having about her since they'd met.

"Man, how stupid are you?" he muttered.

Maybe he should call Shandie and say he was sick or something and couldn't make it…

But like his earlier deliberation about leaving Thunder Canyon, not going through with tonight with Shandie was a short-lived consideration, too.

Because since she'd agreed to go with him he'd been looking forward to the damn dinner just so he could have a little concentrated time with her. And if he wanted to be with her badly enough to make him look forward to this dinner? He wanted to be with her too badly to cancel out now.

"So apparently you're plenty stupid," he answered his own question of a moment before.

But he wasn't going to refuse himself the only thing he'd actually wanted to do in as long as he could remember. He would just make sure to abide by the terms she'd set, he told himself as he turned off the water and reached for his towel.

No strings attached—that was what she'd said. And that was what he needed—and wanted—too.

They'd go to the dinner as friends, and maybe his showing up with her on his arm would be the key to shutting down those freaking sympathetic looks he kept being the recipient of, and Shandie would get to meet some people—everybody would come out ahead.

Yeah, that was another way to look at it.

Then Shandie Solomon would go on about her business and he would go on about his— no harm, no foul, no strings.

Maybe this was actually the best route to take.

Or maybe he was kidding himself.

But for once—and unlike his usual perspective these days—he decided to opt for the better of the scenarios and believe that this evening would accomplish a few good things.

He already knew for a fact that something positive would come of it—he was going to get to see the new blonde on the block for a while tonight. And that was definitely something good.

Good enough to almost make him feel as if things were already looking up....

* * *

"Did you say you were from Denver?"

"I did," Shandie confirmed in answer to the question Dax asked her as he pulled away from her house Wednesday night.

He'd come to her door only a few minutes earlier and won more of Kayla's fondness by giving the three-year-old a set of toy racing motorcycles complete with a track. Then he'd helped Shandie on with her black, calf-length coat while telling her she looked terrific in her gray pin-striped, cuffed trousers and the white angora sweater she'd judged just dressy enough for the evening.

She'd returned Dax's compliment, but it had been an understatement. He didn't merely look nice, he looked jaw-droppingly fabulous in charcoal slacks and a black turtleneck sweater that gave him a man-of-mystery-and-danger sort of edge while still dressing him up, too.

But now that they were on their way, he was making small talk that Shandie thought was designed to conceal that he was very much on edge. And while she didn't wish him any stress or discord from his other relationships, she just hoped his tension wasn't a result of being with her.

"I was born and raised in Denver," she continued. "It's where I've lived all my life."

He smelled wonderful, too, she thought as the scent of a clean, airy cologne wafted to her in the cab of his truck.

"And you just decided to chuck it all and move to Thunder Canyon?" he asked.

"Well, I wasn't really 'chucking it all.' I was a late-in-life baby, and both my parents are gone. Judy is all the family Kayla and I have left, so when she offered me a partnership in the Clip 'n Curl and it meant moving up here, I thought *why not?* Especially since Thunder Canyon is relatively small—it just seemed like it might be a better place to raise a child on my own."

Dax nodded.

"What about you?" Shandie asked to keep the ball rolling. "Are you from here or from somewhere else?"

"Thunder Canyon—born and bred."

"And you've always lived here?"

"I've done some traveling but, yeah, this has always been home. For better or for worse."

"Do you not like it here?" Shandie inquired, wondering if that was what he was implying.

"No, I like it. Well enough not to leave it, I guess."

"Has that been a possibility? Your moving away?"

"It's something I think about from time to time," he said. "But don't let that change your mind about Thunder Canyon—you're right, it is a good place to raise kids. I had a lot of fun growing up here. I think Kayla will, too. If Jack S. gets off her back."

"I don't know. Kayla and Jack S. seem to have a love-hate thing going," Shandie joked.

They'd arrived at the main lodge of the Thunder Canyon Resort by then.

Like a tour guide, Dax informed her that what had begun as a ski resort was now a four-season destination that drew upscale tourists from around the world.

Shandie wasn't surprised that the beauty of the rustically elegant Alpine-flavored gateway to the mountain had become a big draw.

There were parking spots closer to the entrance, but several cars had pulled in just in front of them and Dax seemed to hang back from where they were all headed, choosing a spot behind them.

"Looks like everybody's getting here at

once," he observed, apparently recognizing the cars.

"Then we won't be too early or too late," Shandie said brightly, as if she hadn't noted the more somber note that had edged Dax's comment.

He turned off the engine, removed the keys from the ignition and put them in his pocket, but he made no move to leave the truck. Instead, his gaze was glued to those other cars and the people who were emerging from them without any hesitation.

"Who's who?" Shandie asked as they all seemed to gather to say hello without any knowledge that she and Dax were there watching.

"The tallest guy in the coat that looks like it came straight out of a magazine? That's Grant Clifton. He manages the resort now, which seems right since he's always been driven and ambitious. He's the man to make it be all that it can be."

"And the woman he's holding hands with?"

"Stephanie Julen. Steph, Grant's fiancée. She's our nature girl—more at home on the back of a horse than anyone I've ever known. Next to them—the guy built like a brick wall —is Mitchell Cates. He's the founder and president of Cates International, a company that sells farm and ranch equipment. He caused some trouble when we were kids," Dax said affectionately and clearly with fond memories of the trouble. "But he's pretty serious now. That's Lizbeth Stanton with him…"

Dax's tone had slowly brightened as he'd talked about his friends, and Shandie could tell that he was genuinely fond of them and even proud of their accomplishments and attributes. But that brighter tone dimmed with the mention of the woman Shandie had heard he'd been engaged to.

Was he jealous now that Lizbeth Stanton was with his old friend? Shandie wondered. Or were there harder feelings between him and his former fiancée than he'd let on when he'd said what little he'd said before about her being at this dinner?

But Dax didn't offer anything else on the subject of Lizbeth Stanton, and Shandie didn't think it was the right time to pry.

So, instead, she prompted him to go on by saying, "Next to them?"

"That's Marshall—Mitchell's brother." The warmer tone returned to his voice. "He's a doctor. Sports medicine. He practices at the resort now that it's grown, but he was at the hospital in town before. He's with Mia—she's actually an heiress who came to Thunder Canyon to hide out. That's how they hooked up."

"They look happy," Shandie commented, feeling a twinge for what she'd lost herself as she looked at them standing there with their arms wrapped around each other's waists.

"Russ Chilton is beside Marshall. Russ has a ranch outside of town. He's our good ol' boy. He likes things the way they are, doesn't like that change and progress are not only on the way, they're here. He and Grant have always been as close as brothers. Closer than I ever was with mine..."

Again Dax's tone reflected a darker side that Shandie didn't delve into.

"Is your brother there?"

"D.J." Dax named him. Then he pointed a long index finger in the direction of the entrance to the lodge. "There he is. Looks like he and Allaire are playing host. See them standing in the doorway, waving for everyone to come in?"

Shandie altered her line of vision until she located the couple Dax was referring to.

Even from the distance she could see a resemblance between Dax and his brother, although they were opposite sides of the same coin. Where Dax was all bad-boy good looks, D.J. was pure boy next door.

"He made a fortune selling barbecue sauce after he left Thunder Canyon," Dax was saying. "Then he sank that money into opening a chain of his Rib Shack restaurants. He just opened one here. That's where the dinner is tonight, so I guess that's why he's acting like everybody's coming to his house."

Dax sounded as if that made him reluctant to go through with this, but Shandie wasn't going to give him an easy out by asking if that were the case. Rather, she said, "And Allaire…"

"My ex-wife," he said. "She teaches art at the high school."

Nothing more was offered, and again Shandie didn't think she had a right to delve into it.

"There's a late arrival—well, besides us," she said when the driver and passenger of the car that had just joined the others got out and were greeted by the group.

"Riley Douglas and his wife Lisa," Dax said. "Riley is Caleb Douglas's son. Caleb is as close to the town's patriarch as there is. He's the richest man around, has his hand in just about everything. He owns the resort, but he's turned over running it to Riley now."

"That's different than Grant—what was it, Clifton?"

"Grant Clifton, right."

"Didn't you say he ran the resort?"

"He manages it. He supervises the day-to-day operations, while Riley is still the higher-up."

"And Riley's wife, Lisa? What does she do?"

"She's an animal lover. She's devoted to animal welfare—if there's any suspicion of an animal being abused or neglected, Lisa'll come out with both barrels blazing." He paused, then concluded, "And that's the whole bunch."

For a moment they just sat there silently, watching everyone gather at the lodge's entrance to continue their hellos inside, to shake hands or clap backs, to exchange a hug here and there. It was very clear what a close-knit group it was and how happy they all were to be together. And Dax was making no fast moves to be in on it.

"Well, it looks like this'll be fun," Shandie said with nothing whatsoever to base that on, merely trying to be encouraging.

"Looks like it will be for them," Dax muttered.

Shandie finally decided to concede what she'd been trying to avoid and said, "If you don't want to go, we don't have to."

It took him a long time to answer that, during which he watched his friends, his exes, his brother from the distance and obviously reconsidered.

But then he said, "Nah, we've come this far, we might as well go in."

"Like I said before, you might be sorry if you don't," she said gently to support his decision.

"Yeah," he agreed halfheartedly. "Who knows? Maybe it won't be so bad."

Chapter Four

The drive home from the pre-Thanksgiving dinner was nothing like the drive to it. Where pleasant conversation had filled the truck cab before, afterward there was only silence that made Shandie want to squirm.

In spite of that, she didn't break the silence. The evening had been so bad, and Dax's mood seemed so dark as a result, she wasn't too sure she should.

When Dax pulled into her driveway she half thought he might merely wait for her to get out and just drive away without ever saying a word. It surprised her that he turned off the engine and walked her to her door. But he still didn't speak.

By then, though, she thought she *had* to say something. So as she unlocked and opened her front door she said, "I'm sorry—"

That was as far as she got before her daughter skipped up to the screen dressed in red footed pajamas with a full wig of black hair on her head.

"No! What are you doing?" Shandie blurted out, flinging the screen door open in a panic. "You know better than that!"

An unrepentant Kayla laughed and ran, squealing as she did, "But I'm pitty!"

Shandie hurried inside. "Come in," she called over her shoulder to Dax, knowing it came out more as an order than an invitation and that he probably didn't want this evening prolonged any more than it had to be and wouldn't have accepted the invitation had she extended it. But as it was, she couldn't merely leave him standing on the porch in the cold and she had to get to her daughter and that wig.

"Kayla Jane Solomon! Don't you run away from me! Stop right now!"

"I'm pitty!" the three-year-old repeated.

Shandie followed her to the right of the entryway into the living room, but the little girl had already ducked into the coat closet and slammed the door after her when the babysitter appeared from the kitchen with Kayla's yellow security blanket in hand.

"I just read her a story and put her in bed upstairs. We forgot Blankie so I came down to get it," a wide-eyed Misty explained.

"It's okay," Shandie assured the fifteen-year-old. Then, in a louder voice aimed at her daughter, Shandie said, "I mean it, Kayla. Come out here now!"

Giggles preceded the scant opening of the closet door as the tiny child peeked through the crack. "I'm pitty," she insisted yet again.

"You know you aren't supposed to touch those wigs. Get over here so I can take it off without ruining it."

Her daughter finally complied and stepped from the closet. The black wig was even more askew after the little girl's mad dash. It had slipped too low on her brow and was far enough over her eyes that Kayla had to tip her head far back to peer out from underneath it.

Dax had joined everyone in the living room by then, and Shandie caught sight of him. She was shocked to see that a small smile had eased the dark frown he'd worn since leaving the restaurant at the Thunder Canyon Resort. If Kayla's misbehavior had accomplished it, it was almost worth it to Shandie.

But that still didn't mean she could let the child get away with what she was doing.

Shandie bent over and very carefully removed the wig. "You know you are not to touch these," she told her daughter firmly as she gently set it on an antique table against the wall.

"'Cuz they're the sick ladies' hairs," Kayla responded, reciting by rote what Shandie had explained to her more than once. "But I was bein' pitty."

"You can be pretty some other way, but you never, ever touch these."

Kayla rolled her big blue eyes and reluctantly conceded. "I won't." Then she noticed Dax and cast him a smile. "I played with the motorcycles. Misty helped."

"And then I really did put her in bed," Misty said meekly. "I really did, and I told her to stay there while I came downstairs just to get the blanket."

"I'm sure you did. I know this isn't your fault. It's just something Kayla will do when she gets wound up," Shandie told the teenager as she accepted the security blanket from her.

Then Shandie returned her attention to her daughter and said, "Kayla, go back to bed. I'll pay Misty and then I'll be there to tuck you in."

"I don' wanna go to bed. I wanna play motorcycles with Dax-like-Max-the-dog," Kayla said.

Shandie had to lunge to catch the tyke as Kayla tried to run again.

"Like I said, wound up," Shandie repeated to her onlookers as she settled her daughter on her hip.

"I'll square things with Misty," Dax said. "Go ahead and put Kayla to bed."

Shandie hadn't dated as a single mother and had no idea if it was customary for the man to pay for the sitter. But in case it wasn't, she said, "It's okay, I can—"

"Go on," Dax urged. Then, to Misty, he said, "I saw that you walked down here, but I can drive you home."

"I'd rather walk. I can talk to my…friend on my cell if I do. Otherwise I won't be able to because it's passed my phone curfew at home."

Dax looked to Shandie once more. "What do you think? Is it okay if she walks home?"

"I guess," Shandie said, knowing it was only a few houses up the block.

"Then I'll take it from here and you can get that pint-sized troublemaker to bed," he said, scratching the tip of Kayla's nose with one finger.

"You're positive?" Shandie asked.

"Positive," he answered with no hint remaining of the dismal mood that had crept over him as the evening had progressed.

Shandie finally accepted that he was going to pay the sitter and said to Kayla, "Okay then. Say thank you to Misty for staying with you, and tell everyone good-night."

"I don' wannoo."

Shandie decided against forcing the issue and merely said her own thanks to Misty. "I'd like to keep your number and have you sit again if you would."

Misty seemed relieved that Shandie wasn't holding Kayla's behavior against her and swore she'd stay with the three-year-old any time Shandie asked.

Then Shandie said to Dax, "I'll see you in a few minutes," and headed for the stairs with an overtired and very silly Kayla bidding Dax and Misty giddy good-nights over Shandie's shoulder.

Shandie knew that any more reprimands of the little girl when she was this weary and stimulated at once were likely to result in tears, so she merely took Kayla to the child's room, laid her in her bed and situated the covers around her the way her daughter liked them. Then she gave Kayla the security blanket.

Kayla promptly located her favorite corner of the blanket, poked her index finger into a fold in the satin edging, put her thumb in her mouth and began to stroke her cheek with her satin-encased forefinger.

Shandie shook her head at her remorseless mischief maker, bent to kiss her forehead and said good-night.

"Night," Kayla said around a mouthful of thumb before she closed her eyes.

"I love you," Shandie whispered but Kayla was already asleep.

Shandie kissed her a second time and slipped from the room.

Which then left her in the same position she'd been in before Kayla's comic relief— she was going to have to face Dax.

In the hallway outside her daughter's door, Shandie took a deep breath to bolster her courage and then went downstairs.

Dax was just closing the front door.

"*Is* Misty okay out alone this late at night?" Shandie asked, hoping she hadn't made a mistake in letting the teenager walk home.

"There isn't much crime in Thunder Canyon, and I see her walking to and from friends' houses all the time. But I just kept an eye on her. She's letting herself in right now."

Shandie nodded, appreciating that he'd been conscientious enough to watch the young girl get home safely.

But then she realized they were back where they'd started—in silence.

"Can I get you a cup of coffee or a drink?" she offered.

"No, thanks. I've had enough for one night."

Enough of more than libations, she thought he meant. But she recalled the fact that he'd been smiling at Kayla and even though he wasn't smiling any longer, his expression wasn't as dour as it had been on the way home. She thought that if his spirits had been lifted by her daughter's antics, maybe she could cash in on that to follow through with the apology she'd begun at the door.

"Why don't we go in and sit down?" she said, not waiting for an answer before she led the way into the living room.

Shandie had decorated in warm brown, rust and cream colors with a few genuine antiques mingled with furniture that aimed for comfort. She sat on one side of the brown velvet sofa made up of cushions as fluffy as pillows.

Dax didn't hesitate to follow her—something she accepted as a good sign—or to join her on the couch, at the opposite end.

Shandie took another deep breath, sighed it out and finally said, "Okay, I was wrong. So-o-o wrong. You probably *wouldn't* have been sorry if you had missed that dinner tonight."

"Ya think?" he said facetiously.

But his tone had more of a note of joking to it than of blame, and she took that as a good sign, too.

"Everything just kind of tightened up when we walked into the room," she said, deciding that she might as well not pretend she hadn't noticed the response that had been so strong it had nearly been palpable.

"I know. That's how it's been for a while now."

"Why? I mean, it's not my place to get into it, but you and your brother barely—barely—acknowledged each other from different corners of the room, you never even said hello and everybody made sure to keep you from getting anywhere near each other. Plus, your friends tiptoe around you. What's up with all that?"

"There's...stuff," Dax said with a wry laugh.

"What stuff? Start with your friends—are you a time bomb they're afraid will go off any second?"

"I don't think it's quite that bad," he said. "It's more that while they've all had one success after another and found their paths, I... haven't."

"Your business isn't doing well?" Shandie asked.

"I haven't had a customer all week," he said. He shook his head and shrugged. "It's more than that, though. I'm just not...into it. Into business. It isn't what I want to be doing. What I'd planned to be doing."

Shandie kicked off her shoes so she could pull her feet underneath her on the couch and face him. "What did you plan and want to be doing?"

Dax pivoted enough to stretch an arm along the top of the sofa back. "I was supposed to be racing motorcycles. That was all I ever wanted to do, what I was sure I would do. At least until I got too old for it. I figured then—and only then—I'd open a shop like I have now. But I thought I'd be a lot older than I am before it came to that. That I'd be ready to devote my energy to business—building it, running it, making a success of it. That it would be my choice—the *next* stage of life, somewhere far down the road."

"So why *are* you in it now? Did you try racing and not make it?"

"No, I made it. I raced professionally for seven years. From right after high school until not quite two years ago. My name'll still pop up here and there when it comes to winning streaks—I had some of the best. I was the man to beat…"

"Wow," Shandie said, impressed despite a note in his voice at the end that she couldn't quite pinpoint. Something bittersweet, maybe? "And you liked doing it?"

"Loved it. It was…" He shook his head, his almost-black eyes rolled toward the ceiling, and it was clear in every line of his handsome face just how much he'd loved motorcycle racing. "It was great," he finally finished, obviously understating what he couldn't find words grand enough to describe.

"Something big must have happened to make you quit," she said.

"Something pretty big—I blew a tire and hit a cement wall. Smashed half the bones in my body, broke my spine in three places. Everybody was amazed I lived through it."

"Wow," she repeated, this time in dire awe.

"Yeah," he agreed. "I spent months in a hospital, more months in a rehab facility. I did everything any doctor, any physical therapist, any trainer told me to do. I worked out, I lifted weights…" he chuckled "…I even did yoga to see if I could get back to racing shape—"

"You look like you're in shape," Shandie offered, to explain the fact that she was giving him the once-over in search of any residual clues to his accident. And in hopes that he wouldn't realize how much she was admiring the view.

"I'm healthy," he said. "I feel fine. I'm strong again. Everything works the way it's supposed to. But my spine has pins in it and won't let me bend over the bars the way I need to, to race. Plus, I somehow dodged the paralysis bullet the first round, but no one I talked to left me with any doubts that another injury to my spine would leave me in a wheelchair. And motorcycle racing is hardly a low-risk occupation. So in the end…that was it for me."

"And your plans for later in life had to be moved up," Shandie concluded.

"Yep."

"And your friends all know this isn't how you wanted things to play out. They know how much you miss racing. They feel bad for you. They know you can't do what you want most *to* do at the same time they're all achieving their own goals."

Dax sighed. "I suppose. There's been some personal stuff, too. A marriage that ended and a really dumb engagement. And I probably haven't been exactly…chipper…about it all."

Even though she was interested in the story of that marriage and engagement, Shandie opted for not prying into them right then. "Sometimes you just can't be chipper about the hand you get dealt," she commiserated instead, recalling some dark days of her own. "It's nice of your friends, though, not to want to flaunt their own successes and make you feel worse."

"Nice, but not a lot of fun for them."

Shandie couldn't argue that so she moved

on. "What about your brother? What's going on there?"

Dax gave her a semblance of a frown. She knew it was only a semblance of one because she'd seen enough of the real thing tonight to tell the difference. But even if she hadn't, one side of his sexy mouth was also tilted upward to give him away before he said, "Don't be shy, Shandie. If you're curious, just ask."

Shandie grinned at him. "I did. Don't forget, I hang out with a three-year-old—I might be picking up some of her habits. But still, I earned an answer—I suffered through that dinner tonight, too, you know."

"True," he conceded, and she was grateful that he didn't throw it up to her that she had been behind the push for him to go in the first place.

"The *stuff* between D.J. and me goes a lot further back than the wrong turns my life has taken. You couldn't say we were ever close."

"Not even as kids?"

"We fought like two mad dogs," he admitted. "It's a wonder we lived through it."

"How far apart are you in age?"

"Only a year—he's a year younger than I am. But we were different growing up—we liked different things, did different things—

and there were some family dynamics that were a problem."

"Family dynamics?"

"Our mother died in a car accident when we were little—I was eleven, D.J. was ten. I loved her, of course. She was my mom and it was terrible to lose her. But you could say that I was closer to Dad, and D.J. was closer to Mom, so I think Mom's death hit D.J. harder, maybe?" Dax said, apparently feeling his way along, as if even he wasn't completely clear about the details of what had gone on inside his brother's head.

"I don't know," he confessed when he continued. "I just know that I went on being really close to Dad. We were both into motorcycles and racing. He bought me my first bike, taught me to ride, got me into some amateur races as soon as I was old enough and good enough. We worked on the bikes together—we spent a lot of time at it. We just…we were a lot alike, and that was never more true than when it came to being motorcycle-crazy—"

"And your brother?"

"D.J. couldn't have cared less about motorcycles or racing. He sure as hell never seemed to want in on any of it."

"So he was just left out?" Shandie asked, feeling some sympathy for Dax's brother.

Dax scratched a spot just below his ear-lobe with a long index finger, his square brow pulled into deep furrows. "That sounds bad. It wasn't like we purposely excluded him or anything. D.J. *could* have been right there with us if he'd wanted to be. I know Dad wished D.J. wanted to be. But D.J…. It just wasn't his thing."

Shandie didn't think Dax deserved any blame for his brother's not sharing in what Dax and their father had had in common, but she did think that he felt a little guilty for how the *family dynamics* had evolved.

Then, with what seemed like reluctance, he said, "And then there was Allaire."

"D.J.'s new wife."

"My *old* wife," Dax said under his breath.

There had been some talk at the dinner about D.J.'s and Allaire's recent marriage, but Shandie didn't make any comment because she didn't know how sore a subject it might be with Dax. She merely let him go on.

"I don't have the details or the timetable, but I guess D.J. was in love with Allaire when we were all in high school—and maybe even earlier. Not that I knew that, because I didn't."

Dax was quick to defend himself. "If I had… Well, there were a lot of girls. I might not have gotten in his way with Allaire if I'd known. But I didn't have a clue he wanted her. Everybody there tonight? We were all friends and none of them knew, either. D.J. kept it top secret—that was just like him, Mr. Suffer-In-Silence."

"But he did have a thing for Allaire, and you ended up with her," Shandie said, piecing it together.

"Yeah," Dax said regretfully. "I didn't catch on to how he felt until my own wedding to her." Dax shook his head as if he still couldn't believe it. "Everything was going along great—I *thought*. Nice wedding, good time, everybody seemed happy. Then I looked up as Allaire and I were doing that arms-linked-to-drink-champagne wedding thing, and there over my glass was D.J.'s face. And that was when I knew. It hit me like a ton of bricks. His expression was just…raw…and I knew he was in love with her." Again Dax shook his head, this time as if he still couldn't believe what he'd seen. "My brother was sick in love with the person I'd just married," he said more to himself than to Shandie.

"That couldn't have helped your relationship with him," Shandie interjected.

"Not by a long shot. D.J. left town right after that. I don't think he could stand to be anywhere around the two of us. And things went downhill from there. That was nine years ago, and until he moved back to Thunder Canyon I didn't see him or hear from him more than a handful of times—we'd exchange a card here and there, an e-mail, he came to the funeral when Dad died of a heart attack five years ago, but that was pretty much it."

"What about when you had your motorcycle accident?"

Dax's eyebrows arched. "I was unconscious for four days. D.J.'s face was the first one I saw when I woke up," he mused as if he'd almost forgotten that. "I'm still foggy about most of what went on for those first few weeks after the accident, but I've been told that D.J. came as soon as he heard, stayed at the hospital, made sure I had the best orthopedic surgeon there was to put the pins in my spine, to set the rest of my bones. But when he knew I was going to be okay, he left. So by the time I was really alert to things again he was gone."

"He just couldn't handle being too close?"

Dax nodded. "I'm only now beginning to see that when it comes to D.J., there's been a lot of resentment that I didn't even know was there. I just thought—" Dax shrugged yet again "—you know, that we were different. That he didn't get me, and I didn't get him. It happens."

"But now you're realizing how hard it must have been for him to lose the person he felt closest to in the family, to be odd man out with you and your dad, and then to watch you sail off with the person he was in love with on top of it," Shandie observed.

"Odd man out…" Dax repeated as if she'd said something profound. "Yeah, I'll bet that *is* how he felt. With me and Dad, then with me and Allaire. And everybody else around here, too, since Allaire and I getting married was a big deal and all our friends thought it was great…the way they all think her marriage to D.J. now is great, come to think of it. Anyway, it couldn't have been easy for D.J.…" That seemed to strike Dax as a revelation.

Maybe Shandie should have left him to it, but she didn't. She said, "Did I hear right? Was there really some kind of a physical fight between the two of you not long ago?"

Dax came out of his reverie to aim those intense eyes on her. "Yeah, there was. A knock-down-drag-out brawl. At the opening of The Rib Shack at the resort. It was dumb. A throwback to the old days," he admitted as if he wasn't proud of it.

"I take it there hasn't been a warm brotherly reunion since then, or you wouldn't have needed separate corners tonight," Shandie said.

"No, we've kept our distance. I didn't even go to his wedding. But then I don't think anybody expected me to—there was the fight and he was marrying my ex-wife—their wedding didn't seem like a place for me."

"He's still your brother," Shandie ventured. "He's family."

"The only family I have left," Dax agreed but not in a way that caused her to think he was considering the true weight of that.

"And now he's living in Thunder Canyon again—which is a relatively small place. He's married and reconnected with all your old friends, who are welcoming him back into the fold. Won't it be kind of hard to keep a feud going under those circumstances?"

"Feud? I don't think we're feuding."

"I don't think you're behaving much like brothers, either," Shandie countered.

Dax shrugged once more.

"Oh, don't act as if you don't care," she accused.

"What do you want me to say? That I wish things weren't the way they are? Wishing things weren't the way they are is my middle name."

"But this is something you can do something about."

"I can't make it so that D.J. was as close to Dad as I was. I can't wipe away my marriage to Allaire so he and Allaire could have gotten together before this. I can't change history."

"But you can reconnect with him now. Talk to him. You can make up, put the past behind you and go on from there. That's what I would do if I were you. I wouldn't so easily let go of family. *Any* family, let alone someone as close as a brother."

"Is that so?" Dax said with an amused half smile, as if he'd enjoyed her impassioned rant. "And did you know that when you get riled up like that your eyes sparkle and your cheeks get all red and rosy?"

Shandie was sure her cheeks were getting much more red and rosy at that moment because she could feel herself blush in response to his words.

"I'm not *'riled up,'*" she said anyway.

"You're a little riled up."

"I just think family is important."

"And what makes you think I should be the one to offer the olive branch? Why shouldn't D.J. do it?"

Shandie rolled her eyes at him for that and ignored it. "You've both done things and said things. You have regrets when it comes to him, he probably has regrets when it comes to you. Just let it go and open the door for him to let it go, too."

"Yep, riled up," Dax said with an even wider smile.

"Well, I'm glad I could entertain you," Shandie said snidely.

"I'm glad, too," he countered as if she'd been serious. "It really turned this night around." He glanced at the grandfather clock she had in the corner of the room then, and said, "But I should probably quit while I'm ahead and let you get some sleep."

Shandie scoured her brain for a way to keep him from leaving yet, but she didn't come up with anything and in the meantime Dax stood.

As she followed suit something else occurred to her. "What about tomorrow? I don't suppose you're having Thanksgiving with D.J. Are you going somewhere else?"

"I have a few invitations, but you saw for yourself tonight how things are. I don't think I'll be accepting any of them."

"You're going to spend Thanksgiving alone?"

"It's no big deal," he said.

"With Judy gone, Kayla and I are on our own, too. But I want Kayla to have the traditional day so I have a huge turkey and all the fixings. Why don't you come here?" she asked, unable to help herself.

"That's okay. It's really not a big deal," he repeated.

"Any holiday you spend alone is a big deal, and this way Kayla and I won't feel like we're alone, either."

"You're sure?" he asked, echoing her question to him about paying the babysitter.

"I'm sure. It'll give Kayla the chance to play motorcycle with you," she added as if she wasn't thinking solely of how much she wanted to see him again.

"So we're talking another just-friends-no-strings-attached deal," he said as if he found some humor in that but might also be reminding her of the terms that had allowed them to see each other tonight.

"Right," Shandie confirmed, for some reason feeling slightly let down by that qualification despite the fact that it was absolutely what she should have said herself.

"Okay," he agreed. "What time shall I be here?"

"We usually make a full day of it. When I was a kid I started it out by watching the Macy's parade on television, but I thought tomorrow I'd record it for a little later so there won't be a rush getting up in the morning. We can start that about one—why don't you come then and we can go from there? Unless you just want to have dinner with us..."

"No, I'd like to do the whole thing," he assured her without hesitation. "I'll be here at one. Can I bring anything? Not that I cook, but I could stop and pick up a pie or a can of cranberry sauce or—"

"I have everything. Just come." And even though Shandie loved holidays, she suddenly found that she was looking forward to this one more than she had been a few minutes earlier.

"Sounds good."

Dax headed for the entryway then. As he passed the table against the wall, the wig Shandie had confiscated from her daughter and set there caught his eye.

"What did Kayla say about that?" he asked with a nod in that direction. "Something about it being a sick lady's hair?"

"Mmm," Shandie confirmed. "I make them—wigs."

"You make wigs? Can't they just be bought somewhere?" Dax asked as he moved on to the entry and grabbed his coat from the hall tree there.

"Sure, you can buy wigs a lot of places," she said as she trailed him. "But mine are... special."

"Because they're handmade or something?"

"That and because I use each woman's own hair."

He screwed up his expression so that one side was a sort of a grimace. "Really?" he asked as if the idea put him off.

"I do it for people going through chemotherapy," Shandie explained. "Their hair is going to fall out during treatment, so they cut it before that happens, and I use it to make them a wig. That way they look more natural and feel more like themselves."

"It's a side business for you?"

"Actually, I do it for free," she said quietly because she didn't believe that good deeds should be bragged about.

Dax's eyebrows shot up as he slipped into his coat. "Really? It's like a charity thing?"

Shandie shrugged the way he had so many times this evening. "It's just a little of my time. But the hair is precious and you can see why the wigs—especially one that I'm in the middle of working on—can't be played with by a three-year-old."

The mention of more of Kayla's mischief brought out another smile in him. He really seemed to get a kick out of it.

"Do all hairdressers know how to make wigs?" Dax asked.

"No, it isn't part of that training. I learned to do it after I'd become a stylist. But I work with hair, so it wasn't a giant leap."

And she didn't want to talk about it.

She went to the front door ahead of him and changed the subject. "Tomorrow about one, then? Come hungry, but not too hungry because we won't eat until six or so."

Once he had his coat on he joined her at

the door, studying her from beneath eyebrows angled enough to let her know she'd sparked some curiosity in him.

But like the questions she hadn't asked about his marriage and broken engagement, he didn't pursue the subject of her wig making. Instead, he stopped directly in front of her and merely smiled a small smile.

"You really did turn this night around for me."

"I don't know how—all we've been doing is talking," she said, making light of it.

"Yeah, but it's been nice."

Shandie only nodded her concession to that, feeling the same way but not wanting to admit it. "And tomorrow we get turkey and mashed potatoes and pumpkin pie," she said instead.

"I can't wait," he responded in a soft, silky voice that left her wondering if it was the food he was talking about after all.

It didn't seem to be when those coffee-colored eyes of his were so intently on her, looking into her face as if he could see below the surface.

For her part, she was staring up at him in return, absorbing the sight of those eyes, of that artfully disheveled hair, of that cut and carved bone structure that all worked together to make him dangerously good-looking and hotter than any mortal woman should be expected to endure.

And there they were, at the door, at the end of a date, and while Shandie didn't know if kissing was on his mind, she couldn't think about anything else.

Just friends.

No strings attached.

She reminded herself of the strictures she'd placed on tonight and the fact that Dax had applied them to tomorrow, too. Those limitations dictated that a good-night kiss would be out of line.

Which somehow made it all the more appealing an idea.

But it still shouldn't happen...

Yet when he began a slow move toward her, Shandie did, too. She raised her chin. Heaven help her, she parted her lips...

All to no avail.

Because when Dax kissed her, he didn't go anywhere near her mouth.

He kissed her forehead.

Yes, he lingered there a moment longer than he could have.

Yes, his lips were warm and soft and velvety against her skin.

Yes, his breath in her hair was as rapturous as a tropical breeze.

But she'd wanted a real kiss and she almost groaned in complaint.

She managed not to. Barely. And instead did everything she could to act as if that was no more or less than she'd expected.

"See you tomorrow," she said too cheerfully.

"See you tomorrow," he repeated before he opened the door and went outside, apparently with absolutely no idea that he'd left her unsatisfied.

And the cold blast of air that came in after him?

It was just what Shandie needed to bring her to her senses.

Or so she thought and continued to tell herself as she closed the door, as she turned off the lights, as she went upstairs, washed her face, put on her pajamas and got into bed.

But once she was in that bed?

Disappointment crawled under the covers with her.

Disappointment that as she lay there she

didn't have a toe-curling, knee-weakening, head-lightening kiss to relive.

Even though she knew she was better off without it.

Chapter Five

"Looka me!"

Dax clicked off Shandie's television the moment Kayla skipped into the living room and made that demand.

It was nearly six o'clock Thanksgiving evening, and Shandie had offered him the TV remote control while she took her daughter upstairs to dress for the holiday dinner they were about to share. The house was infused with the luscious aroma of roasted turkey. The snow that had begun early that morning was still falling in big, milky flakes beyond the living room's picture window. There was a fire lazily burning in the fireplace. And after a day of watching the parade, taking Kayla outside to make a snowman and shovel walks, and playing with the motorcycle race set while drinking steaming marshmallow-laden hot chocolate, Dax already thought he'd had one of the best Thanksgivings he could recall. And he hadn't even eaten yet. So when Kayla preceded her mother downstairs and stood before him—proudly preening—he didn't mind at all turning off the football game to pay the three-year-old more attention.

"See my pitty dress?" the little girl said.

"I do. You look beautiful," he said emphatically of the black velvet dress with the lacy white collar and red ribbon bow around her waist.

"New shiny shoes-uz and ties, too," Kayla pointed out, hiking up one foot to display the black patent leather Mary Janes and the white tights that Dax assumed were "ties."

Then she said, "When you goes potty you haves to pull up your underpants first and then the ties—not together—or you gets all bumpy."

Unable to keep from grinning at the information he doubted was meant to be relayed so openly, Dax said, "I imagine so."

"And I gots to wear my locket!" Kayla added, pointing a short, pudgy finger at the small gold, filigreed, heart-shaped pendant dangling from the chain around her neck. "I only gets to wear it on special times when I promise I won' jump or run or anything that makes it break so I don' lose it. Wanna see inside?"

"Sure," Dax said.

"Iss my daddy."

Dax was surprised by how much his interest was piqued by that information.

Kayla's father.

Shandie's—what? Ex-husband? Or not even that?

Dax patted the sofa cushion next to him. "Come on, let's give it a look," he said as if he wasn't consumed with curiosity.

Kayla crawled onto the sofa, kneeling there to face him when she'd accomplished it. "I can' gets it open, you'll have to," she said, holding out the locket for him to do the honors.

The locket was no bigger than Dax's fingertips, and with his nails trimmed to the nub it wasn't easy to pry apart the two sections of the tiny piece of jewelry. But he wasn't about to give up without seeing its contents, so he jammed his almost nonexistent thumb-nail into the crevice that separated the front from the back and managed to open it.

"Tha's him," Kayla said, tucking her chin to her chest to see.

Dax looked at the picture inside the locket, too. It was so small it made him wish for a magnifying glass, but he leaned close enough to make out a face that seemed to have been extracted from a snapshot. The guy appeared to be about his age, a clean-cut blond with an ample smile that showed a lot of straight white teeth. But that was about all Dax could tell from the miniscule photograph.

He wasn't sure what to say about it so he said, "What's your dad's name?"

"Daddy," Kayla answered as if it should have been obvious.

"Makes sense," Dax agreed. He hesitated to ask what occurred to him then, but after glancing in the direction of the entryway and the stairs to make sure Shandie wasn't com-ing, he said, "Where is your daddy?"

"In heaven," Kayla answered simply enough.

In heaven?

Was Shandie a *widow?*

Dax hadn't entertained that possibility,

and it made him even more curious. But not knowing how sensitive a subject this might be for Kayla—although it didn't seem to upset her in the slightest—he merely repeated what she'd said. "Your daddy is in heaven…"

"Uh-huh. Wis the angels. He went there when I wasn't borned yet."

"Hmm," Dax mused, beginning to wonder if that was the truth or something Shandie might have just told her daughter. After all, there were pictures here and there of Kayla from infancy to the present, snapshots of older people Dax had assumed were Shandie's parents and photographs of Shandie and Kayla together. But Dax hadn't seen a single other hint of the guy in the locket—or any guy who looked to have been coupled with Shandie. Which had led him to believe that Shandie was either divorced or had never been married.

Of course she *could* have been a widow, he allowed. A very young widow. It might not be common, but he supposed there was still that chance, despite the lack of memorabilia he could recognize as any sign of a late husband.

But Dax also considered that it might be possible that Kayla's father had balked at the idea of parenthood and rather than let Kayla know that, maybe Shandie had instead decided to say he was dead.

Dax glanced at the locket picture again to see if he could tell if it was genuinely a snapshot or might have been cut out of a magazine or something. But it seemed to be a real photograph.

Shandie a widow?

Happy, upbeat Shandie?

He heard her coming down the steps then, and he closed the locket. "I think it might be time to eat," he confided to Kayla in a quiet voice.

"There's marsh'allows on some orangey stuff called potatoes," Kayla whispered back as if it were a scandalous secret.

"And we know how much you like all things marshmallow," Dax countered with a laugh.

Shandie reached the foot of the stairs and headed for the living room to join them, a serene smile on those lips, which had repeatedly drawn his thoughts today. The same lips he'd wanted to kiss the night before and forced himself at the last minute to avoid.

He was glad she hadn't changed her clothes—she was still wearing the cocoa-brown slacks and the cream-colored sweater she'd had on since his arrival that afternoon, so he didn't feel underdressed in his own dark blue jeans and gray dress shirt. But she'd taken her hair down from its twist at the back of her head and brushed it to fall, silky and free, around her shoulders. He thought she'd also done something to her face because she looked refreshed, and he was reasonably sure she'd applied some kind of lipstick or something.

Dax didn't care about the specifics, he just appreciated the sight that somehow made the room seem warmer the minute she entered it.

He stood, unsure if he was going to be able to take his eyes off her.

"I don't know about you two, but I'm *starved,*" she said then.

"Marsh'allows!" Kayla nearly shouted, not saying anything about having just shown him the picture in the locket.

Dax was glad of that, too. He definitely wanted to know the details of Shandie's past, but he wanted to ask when Kayla wasn't around. Just in case.

The little girl's focus had moved on now, though, because she hopped joyously down from the sofa and tugged on his pant leg.

"Come on! We gitta has candles when we

eat," she announced, trailing her mother to help lead the way to the kitchen.

And as Dax followed behind them he felt something he didn't at first recognize because it had been so long since he'd experienced it.

He felt a little lucky.

Just to be right where he was at that moment.

"Now Dax, too."

"You want Dax to kiss you good-night?" Shandie asked her daughter, who had given that command right after Shandie had kissed the little girl's forehead.

Kayla nodded with her thumb in her mouth.

Dax was standing in the doorway of Kayla's room. He was leaning a shoulder against the jamb, his hands were slung in his pockets and his left hip was jutting out to the side, leaving most of his weight on that substantial leg. At Kayla's request, he'd been there to listen to her bedtime story reading. But Shandie wasn't sure if he wanted to kiss her daughter now.

"How about if I give you two kisses?" she suggested as if that were a treat, hoping it would appease the child.

Kayla stored her thumb on one side of her mouth and said, "No. Dax, too."

"Kayla..." Shandie began on the same note she used to deny her daughter a request.

But just then Dax pushed off the doorjamb and crossed the room on a swagger that was particularly his own. His hands didn't come out of his pockets until he reached the side of Kayla's bed, then he used the left one to press to the wall behind the bed, and the right to grasp the headboard so he could lean far over and kiss her small temple.

"'Night, Kayla Jane Solomon," he said.

Kayla smiled beatifically. "'Night, Dax-like-Max-the-dog."

Then, obviously satisfied to have gotten what she wanted, Kayla closed her eyes and turned on her side, away from both Shandie and Dax.

Shandie didn't say anything about the incident until they were headed downstairs again.

"I'm sorry. She just really seems to like you and—"

"I like her, too. It's okay. And believe me, I've had to do a lot worse than kiss a little girl good-night," he said.

"Really?" Shandie responded as if she was buying the mock intrigue in his tone.

"Oh, yeah. Hundreds of things," he assured her with a cockiness that made her smile as they went into the living room.

"Want another piece of pumpkin pie?" she offered.

"Are you trying to make me explode? No, thanks. Everything was out of this world, and I ate more than I usually do in a week. You didn't tell me you were a gourmet cook."

"I wouldn't say *gourmet...*" Shandie demurred, pleased by the compliment.

They sat on the sofa, not as far apart as they had the night before because neither of them was hugging an end, but not exactly together in the center, either. Dax was clearly feeling at home by then, though. He sat slumped down far enough to rest his head on the sofa back and clasp his hands over his flat middle. His booted feet were on the floor under her coffee table, and his thick thighs were spread far apart—something she had no idea why she'd noticed.

For her part, Shandie tucked one leg underneath her and sat facing his impeccable profile. "Don't forget your leftovers when you go," she reminded him rather than address his compliment any further.

He angled a challenging half grin at her. "Are you kicking me out?"

"No!" she was quick to say. Hinting for him to leave was the last thing she'd intended. It was the last thing she wanted. Much as she knew she shouldn't, she felt as if she'd shared him with her daughter the entire day and had been looking forward to this time alone with him now. "I just don't want you to forget," she added.

"And lose out on a turkey sandwich at midnight? Not a chance."

He drew his gaze away from her then, staring at the blank television screen across from them. "So."

But that was all he said for a moment before he looked at her again, this time from the corner of his eye. "Kayla showed me the picture inside her locket earlier."

"She did?" Shandie said noncommittally.

"She said it was a picture of her dad, and that he's in heaven. Are you a *widow?*" he asked.

"Why do you say it like that?"

"I don't know. I guess when I think *widow,* I think old. And you're not that."

The note of lusty appreciation in his voice

made her smile. And feel good, despite the painful territory they were getting into.

"Yes, I'm a widow," she admitted. "You probably thought I was divorced, right?"

"Or never married."

"With a three-year-old?"

"It happens."

Shandie conceded that with a slight shrug and a nod.

"There's no pictures of him around," Dax pointed out then. "That seemed more like a sign of divorce or a deadbeat dad."

"I can see where you might get that idea," Shandie agreed. "I have a lot of pictures and other things, but I had to take them down and put them away in boxes, one for me and one for Kayla. I take mine out when I have the urge to wallow in the feelings they bring up. For Kayla, it's more a sort of novelty at this point—she asks to see what's in it now and then if she knows I've gone through my box. But for me...I just found that reminders around every corner made it harder to move on. And I was determined that I *was* going to move on."

"Do you *not* want to talk about it? Or him?" Dax asked, giving her the out.

Shandie considered that. But she'd hated

having people treat her the way Dax's friends had treated him the night before—being careful of every word they said to her. She'd been happy to finally get past that, she didn't want to have it start again now because she gave the impression she was on shaky ground. So she said, "I'm okay talking about it if there's something you want to know."

"There is," he said without a pause.

Shandie smiled at his openness. "Don't be shy, Dax," she said, repeating what he'd said to her the previous evening when she'd inquired about what was going on between him and his brother.

"Hey, I told you my stuff. It's your turn," he claimed.

"You told me the stuff about your brother, not about your relationships with your ex-wife or with Lizbeth Stanton," Shandie said.

"We can talk about them another time," he countered as if they were inconsequential.

Shandie didn't believe they were, but she was thinking more about the slight promise he seemed to be making of other times together. Even though that shouldn't have mattered to her.

"So tell me about him—Kayla thinks his name was Daddy," Dax said.

"Well, she's three. I guess that makes sense since that's the only way I refer to him with her," Shandie said with a laugh. "His name was Peter. Pete Solomon." She didn't know if it was off-putting to Dax that her affection for her late husband echoed in her tone, but there it was anyway, and she didn't apologize for it. "He was my first client on my first day as a licensed cosmetologist. I was really nervous and I gave him a pretty bad haircut—which was particularly unforgivable because he'd already told me it was the first cut he'd had since his hair had grown back in after chemotherapy treatment."

"Chemotherapy—there's that word again. First with the wigs, now here. I'm betting there's a connection."

"There is. Going through cancer treatment with Pete, I met a lot of other people having to do it, too. I saw the need and one small thing I could do to help. The wigs are the result of that."

"He had cancer when you met him?"

"He'd had melanoma—skin cancer. Which a lot of people think isn't such a big deal. But it is. It can be. It was his second bout when we met—it had metastasized to his lymph nodes. But he was in remission at that point."

"But with a bad haircut," Dax pointed out.

Shandie smiled at that memory. "He was a good sport about it. He even wanted to pay me, but I couldn't let him. He came back that night when I got off work, though, and insisted he take me to dinner with the money I hadn't accepted for the cut."

"And you went?"

"That surprises you?"

Dax arched his eyebrows. "You weren't scared off by the thought that the guy had already had cancer twice?"

"Well, it *was* just dinner. But he had such a positive attitude that I guess the cancer just somehow seemed less important than maybe it should have been, since that *is* what ultimately took his life."

"If you had it to do over again..."

"I still would have gone to dinner with him that night. I'd still do exactly what I did from then on, too. We didn't have much time together—not even five years—but the time we had was great."

"Even though he was sick?"

"Actually, he was perfectly fine until the last five months. He'd been doing his regular check-ups, he was still in remission..." Shandie shrugged as some of the sadness inevitably washed over her when she talked about Pete. "I guess I kind of thought we were home free. That he would be one of those success stories."

"So you went ahead and got pregnant with Kayla?"

"Oh, no, that isn't how it happened. Pete and I thought that our only option if we wanted a family was to adopt because there's an increased risk of infertility as a side effect of chemotherapy. Even when he proposed, Pete made it clear that he likely couldn't father kids—"

"And you were okay with that?"

"I loved him so much that I was willing to accept it. I was willing to accept anything to be with him—he was just that terrific a person. He was fun and funny and life affirming. He was interested in everything. He saw the good in everybody. He was definitely a glass half-full guy—"

"Sounds like you *and* Kayla," Dax observed.

"I learned a lot about how to look at things through those eyes. And Kayla? Well, she's his." Shandie's voice cracked a bit as emotion welled up, but she tamped down on it rather than allow it to take control.

"So if you thought adoption was the only way you could have a family, Kayla must have been a surprise."

"A big one! Our little miracle—that's what Pete called her, which was a huge relief to me."

Dax frowned in confusion. "A relief?"

"Pete found a lump under his arm in the shower one day, went in to his doctor and this time he didn't get the clean bill of health he'd been getting from his routine physicals. The doctor discovered that the lump was malignant, that the cancer was active again and was pretty widespread already. We'd never used birth control, and it was just as Pete was starting intensive chemotherapy that I realized I was pregnant."

Dax sat up straight and turned to face her, laying a long arm across the top of the rear sofa cushions. "You weren't sure how he'd take the news under the circumstances."

"No, to tell you the truth, I wasn't. He—we both—had a lot on our plate with his health issues and there I was, pregnant. But like Pete's outlook on everything else, he looked at the bright side and he was thrilled. He joked that we could throw up together—him from the chemo, me from morning sickness."

Shandie chuckled slightly. "And believe me, there were days when that was exactly what we did, and when he actually made me laugh about it."

For a moment she was lost in the past and silence fell. Then, quietly, respectfully, Dax said, "So when did he die?"

Tears moistened her eyes but she'd had a lot of practice keeping them from going any farther.

She took a deep breath, exhaled, blinked and said, "I got over the morning sickness, but Pete just got sicker and sicker. The chemotherapy didn't have much effect on the cancer that third time, and in fact it weakened him terribly. His weight dropped, he got pneumonia, then they found that the cancer had spread even more—to his lungs, his brain... He died two months before Kayla was born."

With the hand that was behind her on the back cushion, Dax took a strand of her hair to let it wave around the side of his hand. Shandie had the sense that he wanted to touch her more than that, to comfort her, but that he wasn't certain he should.

"I'm sorry," he said, his deep voice soft, soothing. "That's...about as lousy as it gets."

"It was pretty lousy," she agreed. "I didn't

know how I was going to make it through burying him, having a baby and raising it on my own…"

"So last night, when I told you about the accident, you could relate because you've had some experience with looking up at the underside of hell," he commiserated.

"I know about grieving for a loss. Loss of a person, loss of a life you wanted, loss of what makes you happy."

"It stinks," he contributed, succeeding at lightening the tone because she laughed at his more down-to-earth terminology even as she confirmed it.

"And Kayla never even met her father," Dax said then.

"Not in person. Pete did start making videos of himself for her almost the minute he found out I was pregnant—just in case. She has those in her memory box—"

"Has she seen them?"

"A few. But unless there's animation and bright colors and music and dancing, her attention span is low and she loses interest. So I haven't pushed it. I'm sure when she gets a little older she'll watch them all and get to know her dad and what he was all about. He did make sure not to do any recordings on the days he was sick or as his failing health started to show, so everything is of him looking reasonably healthy and robust—which is good. He was always about so much more than illness that it's important that that's what Kayla gets to see of him."

"What about you? Do you look at the videos?"

Shandie shook her head. "I sat through what I played for Kayla but to tell you the truth, when her attention wandered I was glad to turn them off. I'm thinking that that will get easier later on, but in the meantime it's better for me to work on the present and on building a future than to spend too much time in the past and regretting what isn't anymore. And having Pete in living color on the TV screen? Hearing his voice? Having every detail brought back to mind? That makes it harder to do. Harder to keep my spirits up, to stay seeing the glass half-full."

Dax studied her, his espresso-colored eyes nearly burning into her. Then, after a moment, his mouth barely curved into a smile and he said, "Are these the secrets to how you've come out of it so…"

"Chipper?" She supplied the word he'd used the night before when he'd said that *wasn't* what he'd been since his accident. "I don't think there are any secrets. Or that it's a breeze for anybody to suffer through hard times and come out the other end to go on. I just think that when *lousy* things happen," she said, using another of his words, "you get through it, you grieve, you feel miserable and sorry for yourself, and then you have to start thinking about what you have left, and go from there the best way you can. You do have to figure out all over again what makes you happy when what made you happy before is gone. And for me, one of the biggest things has been the people in my life—Kayla, of course. And friends, and Judy because Judy is my family. Like D.J. is *your* family…"

Dax's eyes narrowed suspiciously. "Are we ending up with a moral for me in this story?"

"Looks like we might be," Shandie said, refusing to be intimidated by him. "You've lost a lot—your mom, your dad, motorcycle racing—but you still have your brother. The two of you aren't kids anymore or rivals for your father's attention or for the same woman. It seems to me that—"

"Yeah, I get it," Dax cut her off.

Shandie got his message, too—he didn't want to hear her say any more about making up with D.J. But she felt compelled to make one more comment. "Don't let your life get too limited, Dax."

Something about that made him give her the one-sided, cocky smile. "Is that what I'm doing?"

Shandie shrugged yet again. "If you let your friends go, if you let your brother go— on top of all that's already gone? Seems like it's shrinking to me."

"Yeah, and shrinkage is never a good thing," he said with a full heaping of bad-boy innuendo that put a lascivious twist to it.

But using that killer charisma to divert them from a more sobering subject also gave her a glimpse at a side of him that made her think he could be a hard nut to crack. No wonder his friends were giving him a wide berth—they probably didn't know how to get through to him or what to do to help him.

He gave her hair a tiny, painless tug and then released it and hoisted himself off the couch.

"Tomorrow's a workday for us both," he said to explain his actions and announce that he was leaving. And probably to make sure he didn't have to talk more about what he didn't want to talk about.

Shandie thought she might have pushed him too far. But there wasn't anything she could do about it if she had, so she didn't try. If he avoided her because of what she'd said, well, that was his choice. And it would save her from herself, she decided, since despite knowing that she really should steer clear of him, she somehow couldn't make herself.

He'd worn a peacoat when he'd arrived that afternoon, and it was hanging in the entryway. He went for it, and once he'd slid it on, his broad shoulders curved forward into a minor slouch as he jammed his hands into the coat's pockets.

"Thanks for today," he said as they moved to the front door.

"Your leftovers!" Shandie nearly shrieked when she remembered. "I'll get them."

She went quickly to the kitchen, unaware that Dax was following her as she did. She didn't realize it until she had the plastic containers out of the refrigerator.

But when she spun around, thinking to rush back to the entry, there he was, standing in the open arc that led to the kitchen, lounging just as he had been in Kayla's doorway earlier—with one shoulder against the wall, his hips at a sexy angle.

"You didn't have to come back here. I would have brought them to you," she said as she approached, expecting him to turn and head for the front of the house again.

He didn't though. Instead, he stood there, essentially blocking her from passing. He didn't take the containers from her, either, leaving her hands full as he looked down at her standing there in front of him, his dark eyes glittering.

"I had a great time," he said, adding to his thanks of a moment before as if there hadn't been a gap.

"So did we. I'm glad you came," Shandie said, feeling something different in the air suddenly. Something that caused everything female in her to make itself known.

"You paid me back for fixing your car by going to that dinner with me last night," he was saying. "How about if I pay you back for today by taking you and Kayla to the Parade of Lights tomorrow night? It's the kickoff to the Christmas season, and you wouldn't want to miss it."

"You don't have to do that," she murmured, wanting to accept and recalling that she'd just been thinking that if things she'd said tonight had scared him off it was all for the best.

"Good, because I'm not big on doing what I *have* to do," he said. "I'd just *like* to do this."

So would she. Even though she knew better.

He's a hard nut to crack, she reminded herself. *That's the last thing you need...*

But Kayla would love to go to the light parade...

Maybe just one more night and then I really will keep away from this guy...

"I wasn't sure it was worth braving the cold for," she said, still hedging because that was the truth.

"You shouldn't miss it," he told her. "The town council sponsors it and everyone in it goes all out. Thunder Canyon will be talking about it for days afterward and you'll wish you had been there."

"Kayla *would* probably get a kick out of it," Shandie admitted.

"Santa Claus brings up the rear—that's what makes it the Christmas kickoff..." His delicious smile was so enticing it was impossible not to be infected by it and smile back.

"Well, maybe..."

"Yes or no," he said, but he made it an alluring ultimatum.

"Okay, yes," Shandie said, finally giving in.

That stretched his smile into a grin. "You won't be sorry."

She hoped not...

He still didn't move from blocking the doorway, though—he stayed right where he was, looking down at her.

"I really am blown away by you. Do you know that?" he said in a deep, husky, intimate voice, raising an arm to lay across one of her shoulders, leaving his hand dangling somewhere behind her but not touching her. "You look all soft and fragile and like...I don't know, like you need protecting. But inside? You're smart and together and strong, and I think you might be able to take on the world if you had to."

"Let's hope I don't have to," Shandie joked because she didn't know what else to say.

"I think Thunder Canyon is lucky to have added you to its population. I think maybe I'm lucky to have you added to my *shrinking* life, too," he said, making fun of what she'd said earlier.

Shandie rolled her eyes to let him know she knew what he was doing in spite of the subtlety. And that only made him grin all the more.

"You're sharp," he said on a laugh.

And then he leaned over enough to kiss her, taking her completely by surprise. Plus, tonight it wasn't only a kiss on the forehead—one minute he was laughing at her, the next his mouth was on hers.

After an instant of shock and a faintly startled rearing back, her lips responded on their own and she discovered she was kissing him in return. Nothing spectacular—well, maybe a *little* spectacular because oh, could the man kiss! But there was some reserve to it, some holding back, in lips that were as supple and adept as they looked but only parted slightly, almost respectfully.

At least until just the scant tip of his tongue flicked out from between those slightly parted lips to hers.

But that was as far as he went before ending the kiss altogether. He straightened up, removing his arm from her shoulder to take the containers of leftovers she was still holding like a schoolgirl holding a lunch tray while the class heartthrob stole a kiss.

She must have looked as stunned as she felt because Dax said, "I'll let myself out." Then, with a nod over her head, he added, "Your refrigerator door is still open a crack."

Shandie turned to see if that was true and when she looked back he was gone, walking down the hallway that ran alongside the staircase with that butt-swaying strut that for no reason she could fathom made her go all mushy inside.

Then he disappeared around the newel post and she heard the front door open.

"Parade's at eight tomorrow night. I'll come down and get you at seven-thirty," he called, just before she heard the door close behind him.

For a moment she stood there frozen in the aftermath of his kiss before she remembered the refrigerator door. As she returned to shut it more securely, it occurred to her that she might just have had a tiny taste of the Dax of days gone by.

And with the feel of his lips still on hers, with the memory of that teasing touch of the tip of his tongue, the image of him walking away on that confident—but still a bit world-weary—swagger, she thought that it was no wonder he'd been one of Thunder Canyon's hottest properties. The man had a certain something, there was no denying it.

She only wished she were immune to it.

Chapter Six

"Lookit! Lookit! It's a piggy wis a big bow!" Kayla shouted gleefully, giggling at the sight of an enormous sow being led on a leash down Thunder Canyon's Main Street.

"Lookit, Dax! Do you see her? Is she Miss Piggy?" Kayla asked.

"Uh, I don't think Dax can see anything," Shandie told her daughter with a laugh when she realized his predicament.

Dax had lifted Kayla to sit atop his shoulders so she could see the Parade of Lights, and she had encircled his head with her arms to hold on. But at that moment, in her agitated state, the three-year-old's grasp had slipped from his hairline to push his eyebrows downward and partially cover his eyes.

Kayla leaned to one side to peer at him and giggled again. "Tha's a funny face," she decreed of the half-pained grimace that her grip had inspired.

But rather than remove her arms, the little girl lowered them even farther so they were completely obscuring his vision.

"Peek-a-boo!" she said.

Shandie grinned at her daughter's antics and Dax's misery but still reprimanded, "You can't stay up there if Dax can't see."

Kayla straightened enough to take her arms from around Dax's eyes as he blinked several times.

"How about you hang on to my ears?" he suggested.

But the little girl ignored him and instead looped her arms under his well-formed jawline like a sling.

"Or there," he said somewhat forlornly.

Shandie laughed again but then said, "She can get down."

"It's okay. I just hope you have insurance to cover the reconstructive surgery I'll need after this," he joked.

"Lookit! Why's that horse gots those funny things in his hair?" Kayla demanded.

"That's his mane," Shandie corrected. "And it's in braids with beads on the ends."

"He's all dressed up to be shown off," Dax said. "A lot of these animals are from the farms and ranches around Thunder Canyon. They're either 4-H winners or they're going to the National Western Stock Show in Denver in January. But we're getting to see them now."

"Can I has beads in my hair like that?"

"I don't think so," Shandie said. Then, to distract her daughter, she added, "Look at this float, Kayla—it's full of fairies all dressed up in lights."

"Can I wear lights when I'm the snow fairy?"

So much for that diversion.

"No, it would be dangerous for you."

"Are you a snow fairy?" Dax asked, apparently interpreting Kayla's question to mean that she liked to pretend to be a snow fairy.

"Me and Mary McDougals are the snow fairies," Kayla responded.

"In the winter program at the preschool," Shandie explained. "And it's Mary McDougal —not McDougals."

"We been practicin' and practicin'," Kayla said, uninterested in the high school flag team that was going by. "'Cuz we has to do it in front of all the mommies and daddies. It's on... When is it on?" Kayla asked her mother.

"Monday night."

"An' my mom has to spray and glitter big clouds and she don' know where she can do it wis'out makin' a mess."

"I've been assigned to make the clouds for the set decoration," Shandie said. "I have to spray-paint them and sprinkle them with glitter, which gets everywhere. Apparently Kayla overheard me talking about it today."

Kayla leaned over and said into Dax's ear, "She don' wanna do it."

It was Shandie's turn to grimace, and she wished she'd been more careful what she'd said within her daughter's hearing. "Don't tell people that," she instructed Kayla. "It isn't that I don't *want* to do it, I just don't know *where* to do it."

"How about at my shop?" Dax offered.

The man was full of surprises.

"The spray paint and glitter will get all over your place, too—I'm sure you don't want—"

"I have a section in the garage where I do some bodywork on the bikes—including paint touch-ups. It's already splattered, so a little glitter won't make any difference."

"I'll need to do it tomorrow night," Shandie warned. "It's the only time I have between work and getting our Christmas tree on Sunday. Are you sure you want to hang around your shop on a Saturday night?"

"I don't have any other plans. You can buy me a pizza for dinner afterward," he said.

This was becoming a relationship of paybacks, Shandie thought.

Not that this was a *relationship*...

But she *did* need somewhere to do the clouds, and it would be a big help to use the open space of his shop.

"If you're sure you wouldn't mind..." she heard herself say before she had more time to consider whether or not it was wise to already be planning yet another evening with him when this one had only just begun.

"I like sausage and olives on my pizza," was his only answer as a marching band came by and made it impossible to hear anything else.

Even though it was past Kayla's bedtime when the parade ended, Shandie gave in to Dax's persuasion to take them to a hole-in-the-wall coffee shop near where his truck was parked. He argued that rather than sitting in the traffic caused by most of Thunder Canyon having come out for the event, they might as well go somewhere warm and have coffee or tea or hot chocolate.

Shandie had seen the small storefront diner but never been in it, and while it was filled to capacity with other parade goers with the same goal in mind, she also knew that it wasn't one of Thunder Canyon's main hangouts. She frequently heard mention at the salon of The Hitching Post and the various options for food and drink at the resort, but besides proximity, she had a sneaking hunch that Dax had chosen this place because they weren't likely to run into his brother or any of his friends.

But after his reaction to her meddling the previous evening, she decided to avoid saying anything about it. Instead she situated Kayla in their booth with the crayons and paper the waitress had provided along with the little girl's cherry-flavored milk, coffee for Dax and tea for Shandie.

"This is a pi'ture for you," Kayla pronounced, sliding a sheet full of scribbles to Dax as the adults sampled their steaming brews.

He glanced at the paper and then at Shandie, obviously unfamiliar with the limited drawing abilities of a three-year-old.

Shandie bailed him out. "What's it a picture of?" she asked her daughter.

"Iss Dax at the parade and tha's Max the dog over there, 'cuz he's brown," Kayla informed them as if they were morons for needing these things pointed out to them.

"It's a work of art," Dax said without any hint of sarcasm.

"You can put it on yur 'frigerator," Kayla told him.

"Can I fold it?" Dax asked.

"Yep. Jus' smooth it out again when yur home," Kayla instructed matter-of-factly as she took a drink of her milk, which left a wide milk mustache.

The grin that erupted on Dax's face as he kept his eyes on her daughter while still folding his picture and putting it in his coat pocket made Shandie look at Kayla, too. When she saw the mustache, she used her napkin to wipe the child's face. Kayla protested, wiggling away from her mother's reach in order to color another picture.

"Were you like this as a kid?" Dax asked her, as if he liked that idea.

"I don't remember how I was at three," she said. "But I do see a lot of what I recall about myself as a kid in Kayla. I had a vivid imagination, too, and I was all girl, which Kayla definitely is."

"Does that mean you were doing your dolls' hair from an early age?" Dax teased.

"Probably," Shandie said, sipping her own herbal tea and drinking in the sight of him across the booth from her at the same time.

He was wearing well-faded jeans, and—from the waist up—layers to keep away the cold. Closest to his hunky body was a white T-shirt. That was underneath a V-neck gray sweater that peeked from behind a hooded sweatshirt zipped to mid-chest. The sweatshirt's hood was pulled above the collar of the ashy-black leather jacket he had on over it all, and the hood was bunched around his substantially muscled neck and behind his head.

His clothes were hardly fashion magazine chic—he was barely more than disheveled—yet he looked so ruggedly handsome she could hardly stand it. It didn't help that, as he sat angled on the booth's seat in his signature couldn't-care-less slouch with one arm casually draped across the seat back, she was ultra-aware of his big hands, one curled around his giant-sized mug of coffee, the other just dangling idly against the tufted vinyl. And she couldn't help wondering how those same hands might feel not so idly cupped to the sides of her face. Or on her bare shoulders. Or lifting her breasts...

"So is that what you always wanted to do? Hair?" he asked.

It took Shandie a moment to tame her wandering thoughts and put herself back into the conversation. Unfortunately, what also registered when she became aware of more than Dax was that her nipples were like twin rocks. And although she was wearing a bra, it was a flimsy one and the turtleneck over it was skintight.

Worried that she was giving herself away, she rested her forearms on the table in front of her and grasped her own teacup with both hands.

"You mean, did I dream of being a hairstylist from when I was a little kid?" she asked in response to his question. "No. Like most girls I was interested in my own hair but doing anyone else's was not what I *always* wanted to do."

"Was there something else that you *always* wanted to do?"

"I was more of a dreamer than a planner. I didn't have an early interest in anything concrete like math or science or motorcycles or anything."

He smiled slyly at her including *his* early interest in that list. "What about when you were a teenager? Were you wild? Did you blow off school and spend more time at the mall? Or were you the editor of the school newspaper and head cheerleader?"

"Somewhere in between and nothing exciting or flashy. I was just one of those middle-of-the-road kids. I made mostly B's for grades, I didn't do a lot of extracurricular activities, I wasn't a cheerleader or class president or anything big. On the whole, what I was really occupied with all through middle school and high school was a boy," she finished with a self-deprecating laugh.

Dax's eyebrows arched. "A boy?" he repeated.

"I told you—I was a dreamer. I was all about romance and love and affairs of the heart."

"But you didn't meet…" He cast a glance at Kayla and clearly didn't know if he should mention Shandie's late husband and Kayla's father by name. "The real deal—" he finally said with a nod in Kayla's direction "—until after high school when you'd gone to work for a living."

"I didn't say it was the real deal—after all, it started when I was barely thirteen. It was just an all-consuming teenage crush."

"On the same guy all the way through school?"

"Jordan Marshall," she said with mock rapture.

"Superjock, captain of the football team, made all the girls go dumb whenever he walked by?"

Shandie shook her head. "We met in seventh-grade home ec. He was short, boxy, bowlegged, wore thick glasses and had a part in every school play—but he particularly liked the musicals."

Dax made a face and laughed.

"Not up to your studly standards, Mr. Tough Guy Motorcycle Racer?" she challenged.

"I guarantee you I do not have standards for studliness," he said through a wry laugh.

"Wus that—stu'liness?" Kayla asked, proving that she was once again eavesdropping on the adults despite the appearance that she was concentrating on something else.

"It just means nice," Shandie lied to her daughter, something else Dax found amusing.

Then he said, "Home ec, huh?"

"My Jordan could make cookies like nobody's business," Shandie confirmed with mock pride.

"I yike cookies," Kayla contributed.

"Me, too," Dax agreed as if he and Kayla were in cahoots. "Maybe we should look up this Jordan guy. He must have made really good cookies because I'm not hearing anything else that would give him six years worth of appeal…"

Dax had said that with an ornery glance at Shandie out of the corner of his dark eyes, goading her.

"Jordan was sweet and funny and I liked him," she said to defend her attraction.

"No," Dax corrected, "you lo-o-o-ved him."

"A crush, I said it was a crush. And I doubt that he'd bake you cookies if you did look him up. I saw him at my class reunion last summer—he's a dentist, married with five kids. I don't think he has time to bake cookies now."

"Damn!" Dax lamented.

"Damn!" Kayla parroted.

"Whoops," he countered, again laughing and obviously remorseless.

"You know better than that, Miss Kayla," Shandie chided her daughter.

Without raising her gaze from her crayon scribbling, Kayla grinned and also said, "Whoops."

"You're a bad influence," Shandie told Dax.

"So I've been told," he informed her, still without regret. Then he said, "How come you didn't end up with home ec man?"

"It really was just one of those young-love things. We were always breaking up and making up and breaking up, and even though we swore we'd make it work long distance when he went away to college, it fizzled. Neither of us ended up with broken hearts or anything. By then, I guess it had just run its course—we'd grown up, grown out of it."

"Was *that* when you discovered the joys of hairstyling?"

"I went to college, too, right after high school, close to home. But only for a semester. I didn't know what I wanted to do—or be—and it seemed unfair to have my parents paying tuition until I figured it out. So I quit and then sort of looked around. My mother was a stylist. And Judy. And it occurred to me that I liked it, too."

"And the rest is history," Dax decreed with his face tilted toward the coffee mug that was on its way to his mouth, looking up at her from beneath eyebrows that were none the worse for wear in spite of Kayla's abuse at the parade.

He finished his coffee, and since Shandie had drained her tea and Kayla wasn't terribly interested in the second half of her milk, Shandie said, "The rest is history and I think this night has to be history now, too. It's getting late and Saturdays are killers at the salon. I should get Kayla home to bed and head there myself."

Dax nodded and aimed his next question at her daughter. "What do you say, Big K? Ready to go home?"

Kayla ignored him, unaware that she was *Big K*. So again Shandie stepped in.

"Come on, Kayla. Time to leave."

"I don' wannoo!" the overly tired three-year-old complained.

"I know, but we have to," Shandie said, beginning to put the little girl's coat on.

Dax paid the bill and they were in his truck

with Kayla firmly buckled into her car seat between them.

There were still a lot of people milling about the streets of Thunder Canyon, but Dax's plan to avoid traffic had paid off and they were back at Shandie's house before the truck had even warmed up. Still, that was all the time it took for Kayla to fall fast asleep.

"Why don't you let me carry her in, in the car seat, and you can put her to bed from there?" Dax suggested when he'd pulled into the driveway.

Shandie agreed to that and as Dax put the parking brake on and left the engine running, she got out the passenger side.

"Go on up and open the door so she doesn't have to be out in the cold for too long," he advised when he'd rounded the truck's front end.

Shandie did as she was told, and he rushed her sleeping child inside and upstairs to Kayla's bedroom with Shandie following behind.

"Just leave the seat on the floor," she whispered when they got there.

Dax did just that and they both crept silently out of the little girl's room again.

Shandie had closed the front door behind them when they'd come in but with his truck still running, Dax clearly wasn't expecting an invitation to stay and he went right back to the door.

"Thanks for tonight," Shandie said as they both reached it. "You were right. The parade was something to see and I'm glad we didn't miss it."

"*I'm* glad you came," Dax said with one of those great, capable-looking hands of his on the door handle. "Do you want to just come through the utility room tomorrow after the salon closes to do your paint-and-glitter thing?"

Shandie had forgotten about that. Of course, at that moment the next day wasn't on her mind—she'd been thinking about how gorgeous his eyes were and how when he looked at her the way he was right then it gave her hot flashes.

But he *was* thinking about Saturday and she had to, too.

"That would probably be the easiest," she answered. "The clouds were precut—thank goodness—and they're still in the trunk of my car from when my *recruiter* gave them to me today after school. I'll just leave them there until I finish for the day and then bring them over to your place. If you're still sure—"

"I'm sure. I'm already counting on that pizza you're treating me to afterward," he said with a slow, teasing smile that made something flutter deep inside of her.

"Besides," he continued, "like I said, I didn't have any other plans. And I have fun with the two of you."

He said that last part as if it surprised him, and although Shandie was reasonably sure that had more to do with his own self-admitted brooding of late and being surprised that he could have fun doing anything with anyone, she pretended to take personal offense. "And here we were trying to bore the pants off you."

His smile eased into an evil grin and he glanced down at his jeans. "Sorry, still on. But if you *want* them off..."

"No, that's okay," she said as if he were serious and needed stopping, acting as if the one glance of her own at his jeans-encased legs and the bump in his zipper hadn't sent those flutters in her into a frenzy. "Don't forget the motor is running on your truck," she added to remind him, not happy to discover that her voice had taken on a breathiness.

His grin got even more wicked. "That's

not the only motor that's running," he said, his own voice octaves lower, deeper, huskier.

Without removing his right hand from the door handle, he raised his left to the back of her neck, leaning forward and pulling her toward him all at the same time to cover her mouth with his.

Unlike his good-night kiss of the evening before, Shandie had seen this one coming. Or maybe she'd just been willing it to happen by thinking about that other kiss—and wanting another.

Not that this was just *another* good-night kiss like its predecessor. This was a kiss with a capital *K*.

His supple lips were parted from the start, enticing hers to part, too, as she kissed him back.

This kiss was firm, commanding, confident, shouting that regardless of what sort of self-doubts he might have in any other area, he didn't have any at all there.

He towered above her, tall and strong, and she thought that if her weak knees buckled beneath her, that single hand at the back of her head could probably hold her up. Yet she found her hands drawn to the solid wall of his chest to steady herself, anyway.

Too, too many layers of clothes, she thought, sorry that anything more than a mere shirt or a sweater kept her from him. But still the kiss was the thing and as his mouth opened wider over hers she was drawn from any other thoughts to that.

The tip of his tongue made itself known again then. But also unlike the previous night, it didn't only jut out in a quick tease. This time it traced the sensitive inner edge of her lips with enough pressure to urge her mouth to open wider, too.

Shandie didn't put up any resistance—not to his persuasion to make way for his tongue to weave its way into her mouth, and not to his bringing her in closer to him. So close that her head was far back in the cradle of his hand. In fact, not only didn't she resist, she met his tongue tip-to-tip and matched him circle for circle, joust for joust, lingering for lingering...

It had been a long time since a man had kissed her like that. A long time since she'd even thought about being kissed like that. But it was nice to know she hadn't forgotten how. Nicer to have it happening again. With Dax.

Dax, who was the first man who had made

her *want* it to happen again. Dream of it happening again. Long for it to...

But his truck was running.

And Kayla was upstairs, still in her coat, in her car seat.

And that kiss was so good it was rousing other things in Shandie that shouldn't be.

That couldn't be...

So push him away, she told herself.

But instead her hands massaged his chest much as his fingers were massaging the back of her head.

His mouth opened wider still and so did hers.

His tongue became even bolder.

And so did hers.

His hand left the doorknob and his arm came around her, pulling her against him, bending her backward with the force of that kiss that was fast becoming more a beginning of something than a simple ending of the evening they'd just spent together.

That was when Shandie did manage to push against Dax.

Okay, so maybe it was more a gentle pressure that could have just as easily been construed as an attempt to press through the layers of clothes he had on. But he got the idea.

He kissed her once more with lips only half-parted, then a final time as if taking just one more taste of a forbidden fruit.

Shandie opened her eyes, finding his opening, too, but lazily even as that sexy, succulent mouth curved into another smile.

"Damn running motor," he said in a gravely voice.

"The truck's or yours?" Shandie asked in a scant whisper because that was the most she could muster.

"Both," he whispered in return.

Then he let go of her and actually did open the front door, flinging it enough to bump the hall tree behind it.

"See you tomorrow night," he said on his way out.

"Okay," Shandie countered, wishing afterward that she'd come up with something better.

But actually she knew she was lucky to have managed that when that kiss had left her brain foggy and the rest of her just a puddle of yearning.

Not until she saw Dax's truck pull out of her driveway did she even think to close her door or recall that her daughter was in need of being put to bed upstairs.

But, once she had closed the door, she stayed there for a moment and took a few deep breaths.

It was as if Dax had flipped on some kind of bright light inside her, and she didn't want to go to even her sleeping child until she could tone it down.

Or at least pull an imaginary curtain around it.

Because what that bright light seemed to be was that part of her that didn't have anything at all to do with being a mother.

What he'd turned a bright light on was that part of her that had gone into hibernation somewhere along the way when Pete had become too ill for more than hand-holding and chaste good-morning and good-night kisses. That part of her that had been left in hibernation as she'd grieved for the man she'd loved, as she'd dealt with a newborn, as she'd learned not only to be a parent, but a single parent.

Suddenly that part of her wasn't hibernating anymore. It was awake and alive and recharged. And desperately wishing that Dax was still there.

Still kissing her.

Maybe taking her beyond just kissing.

And it didn't seem as if she should go up to Kayla until it was back under some kind of wraps.

But even as Shandie worked at that with a few more deep breaths, with her eyes pinched closed as if that would help, she also knew that calming that formerly hibernating part of her didn't mean putting it to sleep again.

Yes, she was courting danger to have that re-awakening caused by bad boy, brooding, adrift Dax Traub. But it still felt good—really good—not to have any portion of her slumbering.

It felt almost as good as kissing him had felt.

Which was something else that she knew had to be contained, controlled, not allowed to just run rampant.

But with a little containment, a little control, maybe she *could* have that simple flirtation.

Because she didn't want to completely put an end to it any more than she wanted to put any part of herself back into hibernation.

Chapter Seven

"I yike Dax," Kayla informed Shandie as Shandie tucked her into bed on Saturday evening.

"I know you like Dax," Shandie said.

"He's funny."

"He made you laugh all night, didn't he?"

It was true—the entire time Shandie had spray-painted and glittered the clouds for Kayla's preschool program Dax had entertained the three-year-old.

"He putted my French fries up his nose," Kayla said, laughing at the memory.

Shandie made a face. "Yuk."

"We din't eated those ones," Kayla said as

if her mother were dim. "And he letted me sit on the big red motorcycle, and he gived me a horsey-back ride, and—"

"I know everything you did, I was there," Shandie reminded her, to cut this short so she could do some freshening up before Dax arrived with the pizza he and Shandie were to share for their dinner. Kayla hadn't been able to wait until this late to eat and had had fast food at the motorcycle shop.

"Can Dax be my boyfriend?" Kayla asked as she situated her security blanket just so.

That alarmed Shandie. The last thing she wanted—or would let happen—was for her daughter to become too fond of someone who could remove himself from their lives at any time.

"No, Dax is too old to be your boyfriend. And you're too young to *have* a boyfriend."

"Is he your boyfriend?"

"No, he's not my boyfriend, either," Shandie said emphatically. "He's just a plain friend." If the kissing they'd done the past few nights didn't count… "He's just a plain friend we have for now," Shandie qualified.

"Not a forever friend?" Kayla asked, picking up on that qualification.

"Maybe he will be a forever friend, or maybe

not," Shandie hedged. "Sometimes people are friends forever and sometimes they're friends for a little while and then they get busy with other things or something changes, and you don't see them so much anymore. You don't count on them."

"Like one-two-free counting?" Kayla asked, confused.

"No, like…"

How to explain this…

Shandie tried. "Like, we had fun with Dax tonight, but if we didn't see him again nothing would be any different for us—we'd still have fun and go places and do things just the same."

"Why wouldn't we see him again?"

The three-year-old mind.

"That doesn't matter. What matters is that you know that it's okay to have fun with Dax as long as we don't count on him *always* being around."

Kayla shrugged the tiny shoulders in her flannel pajamas. "Okay. But for now we can play with Dax and he can be our friend even if he isn't a forever friend," the little girl summarized.

"Right, for now we can see Dax," Shandie confirmed.

"Good, 'cuz I yike him."

Which brought them full circle, and Kayla put her thumb in her mouth and closed her eyes.

Shandie kissed her daughter good-night and whispered, "Just don't like him too much…"

"'Cuz he's jus' a friend for now," Kayla repeated through a yawn, her eyes never opening.

But her daughter's easy acceptance of what they'd just talked about reassured Shandie that Dax hadn't gained any great importance to Kayla. And that was something Shandie was glad of.

She'd watched Dax with Kayla tonight, and on top of seeing how much her daughter had enjoyed him, Kayla's comment just now could have been a warning. But as it was, Shandie thought it had been an opportunity to put things into perspective. To make sure the child grasped that Dax was likely only around for the time being.

Because as long as Kayla wasn't relying on anything more than that, and Shandie herself was aware that any relationship with Dax was destined to be short-lived, it didn't seem as if she was doing any harm to allow him to be a part of things. For now.

Of course, there was the danger that Kayla *could* start to have stronger feelings for Dax or count on him, Shandie reminded herself. But as she changed out of the slacks and shirt she'd had on all day and quickly climbed into a pair of jeans and a white turtleneck sweater that clung to every curve like a second skin, she swore that she would watch out for that. That she would absolutely keep an eagle eye out for any indication that her daughter might be coming to think of Dax as anything more than a passing acquaintance. Because if there was a single sign, that would be it for Dax Traub around here. She would never—ever—risk Kayla's getting hurt. And certainly she recognized that when it came to appeal, Dax was a high risk for both her *and* Kayla. After all, the man just had so much…

Well, so much of everything that was hard not to like. He was smart—and a little smart-alecky in a way that came off more as wit than as anything negative or insulting. He was a great listener—he even paid attention to Kayla's rambling stories. He was patient. Even-tempered—although there *had* been that fight with his brother, but Shandie hadn't seen any indications of a short fuse. He not only had a sense of humor, he could even muster up a genuine laugh for Kayla's silliness. He was just cocky enough to give him an edge. He was never boring. The man had magnetism. And he could be a lot of fun—for both of them.

So, yes, there was a risk of Kayla's getting to like him more and more. Of Kayla's falling under his spell and forming a bond with him that, when it was broken, could hurt the little girl.

But until there was any indication that that might be happening?

"It's okay if I spend a little time with him," Shandie told her reflection in the bathroom mirror as she freshened her mascara and blush and took her hair down from the clip that had held it at her crown since that morning.

It was okay if she spent a little time with him because she didn't have any illusions about him—that's what she'd decided during a long, sleepless night of being stirred up by that good-night kiss. And that was the conclusion she came to again now. She knew that he was in some sort of funk that he needed to work through, she knew that he didn't have the best reputation when it came to women, she knew that he was a really bad bet for anything long-term or serious. And with all of that firmly in her sights, she also knew better than to invest anything emotional in the relationship.

But that didn't mean that she, like her daughter, couldn't just have some fun with him, too. It only meant that she needed to be careful and keep her eyes wide open.

Shandie flipped her head upside down so she could brush her hair from the nape to the ends.

"Eyes wide open," she repeated to herself when she flipped upright again to finger-comb her hair so the layers fell just right and had some definition.

Then she applied a light lipstick that was guaranteed not to come off and surveyed the whole picture.

The sweater was really tight. And there was no room to spare in the jeans, either.

Maybe she should change in favor of baggier clothes…

Caution probably dictated that she should.

But that part of her that Dax had awakened the night before still had a hold over her, and she just plain didn't want to go with baggier clothes.

She could be careful and keep her eyes wide open in tight clothes, couldn't she?

Sure she could.

And when the doorbell rang just then, it seemed like confirmation that she should answer it just as she was.

So that was what she left the bathroom to do.

Swearing to herself along the way that she wasn't trying to entice Dax Traub.

But knowing just the same that what she was wearing was a cashmere and denim invitation to dance....

It occurred to Shandie as she and Dax cleaned up their pizza mess in her kitchen an hour later that she wasn't the only one of them to have changed clothes. He'd said that he needed to run by his place before he picked up their pizza, and Shandie had assumed he'd wanted to shave off the scruffy five o'clock shadow that she'd found very sexy.

But when he'd shown up at her door she'd known instantly that he'd showered, too. He'd smelled of soap and had a just-scrubbed look to him, plus she could spot freshly shampooed hair a mile off. He'd also put on a clean shirt, or sweater actually, because while he'd been wearing a work shirt before, he'd replaced it with a heathered-gray Henley sweater.

But it had taken her until after they'd eaten—as he was bending slightly over her kitchen table to wipe crumbs into his hand— to notice that the jeans he was wearing now were not the same jeans he'd had on at the shop.

Both were faded denim so there wasn't a clue in the color, but where the pair he'd worn earlier had had some sag in the seat, what he had on now followed the arch of his derriere of perfection to a *T,* and left no question about the density of thighs any weight lifter would have envied.

If her clothes were an invitation to dance, she thought, his were an invitation to sin. And Shandie, for one, had an inordinate urge to slip her hands into his rear pockets and squeeze.

Maybe, she decided, she'd better do something to help aid the cause of keeping her eyes wide open. And while she was at it, she'd get some of her curiosity about him satisfied, too...

"I'll finish up in here later," she said, needing to clear her throat to reach a normal tone and cancel the effects of that look at him from behind. "Let's go sit in the living room."

"Whatever you say," Dax agreed, and they left the kitchen.

When they both sat on the couch tonight, it was smack-dab in the center and close enough that when Shandie turned to sit facing him and pulled one leg up onto the cushion, her shin ran the length of his thigh.

It was purely accidental, and she told herself to move. But the heat of him almost immediately seeped into her, and something about how nice it was kept her glued there, pretending she didn't even notice.

"So, thanks to you, I got to be the subject of gossip at my own shop today," she told him.

"Uh-oh. How did that happen and what'd I do?"

"Two of the other girls' clients—who didn't know who I am or that I was within hearing distance—were wondering if I was the next Lizbeth Stanton."

Dax pinched his eyes shut, and his face scrunched into an exaggerated grimace. "This can't be good," he said to himself. Then he opened his eyes, relaxed his expression and said, "Uh-huh," as if he wasn't having any reaction at all.

Shandie laughed at him. But tonight she was determined, and so she refused to be diverted. "I told you about Pete and about my high school sweetheart. I think that makes it your turn."

He looked at her with confusion.

"I want to know about your *personal stuff*," she said, referring to something he'd told her a few days ago when they'd talked about his racing history and his problems with his brother—some of which had stemmed from Dax's marrying the woman D.J. loved. "You said there was a marriage that ended—to your brother's new wife—and a really dumb engagement. And while I've picked up bits and pieces about them, I want to know the real stories—which, I assume, will lead to the comparison between me and Lizbeth Stanton."

Dax made a face that was even more pained. "You really don't want to hear this."

"I really do. Especially when I'm being gossiped about." And before he could dodge the bullet any more, she added, "Start with the marriage."

He made yet another face to show his reluctance, slumped down on the sofa and raised both arms to clasp his hands behind his head before resting back against the cushion.

Then he glanced—or maybe glared—at her from the corner of his eyes. "Allaire," he said on a sigh. "She was *my* Mr. Home Ec— one of those young-love things, isn't that what you called it?"

"I didn't marry *my* Mr. Home Ec," Shandie pointed out. "So yours must have been more than that."

"Yeah, but that's how things started between Allaire and me—in school. She was a grade behind me—in D.J.'s class—but actually a year younger than D.J. and two years younger than me. She was a whiz kid, skipped two grades in elementary school. But even though she was younger, she was still everybody's dream girl."

"She *is* pretty," Shandie said, recalling the other woman from the week before.

"It's not only looks. She's always been an overachiever. She shines at everything she does. She's creative, accomplished, talented—"

"As much golden girl as dream girl," Shandie said before he went on listing the other woman's attributes and made her feel inferior.

"The golden girl—yeah, that was said of her, too," Dax confirmed.

"So she was the one everybody—including your brother—wanted, and you got her," Shandie said.

"Yep."

There was a combination of satisfaction and regret in that single word.

"Did you *want* her or was it a competition thing? Did you just like being the one to win out over everyone else?" Shandie asked, wondering at his tone.

"Oh, I wanted her. It was the young-love thing, remember?"

Admitting to his feelings for Allaire seemed to embarrass him.

"Did you genuinely love her?" Shandie asked, not letting him slide.

"Sure."

"But you don't sound so sure."

He shrugged. "I know some people find their life mate when they're that young and it's the real thing and it lasts *because* it's the real thing. But for Allaire and me? It felt like the real thing and I guess, for then, it was—"

"But it didn't stand the test of time," Shandie guessed.

"We were dumb kids with stars in our eyes. We didn't even know ourselves completely, let alone each other. For my part, I went in with this idea that I would do the whole motorcycle thing and she'd follow me around from race to race like my own private cheerleader or sidekick. It never occurred to me that that might not be what she had in mind for herself—"

"You didn't talk about it?"

"Like I said, we were kids Even though I was twenty-one by the time she graduated and we got married, I wasn't a really mature twenty-one. And she was only eighteen. There was a lot more heart and hormones at work than smarts. We just wanted to be together, our friends were all for it because they thought it was a storybook romance, and away we went—swept along on the whole young-love thing."

"But then there was the reality of marriage."

"And my being on the racing circuit and Allaire not wanting to be just my ride-along pep squad, wanting to carve out something for herself, and… What can I say? The mar-

riage suffered, deteriorated. The longer it
went on, the more she was going her way
and I was going mine, until there wasn't anything in the middle. By the time it ended, it
just seemed to me that it was stupid to have
gotten married in the first place. That if we
had done what you and Mr. Home Ec did—
gone off on our separate pursuits *before* getting married—we probably never would have
found ourselves at the altar at all."

But he wasn't laying blame, and Shandie
was glad of that. Had he put his ex-wife totally at fault and taken none of the respon-
sibility for himself, she would have thought
less of him. As it was, she respected that he
was admitting to his part and not condemn-
ing Allaire, either.

"So you got divorced," Shandie said to en-
courage him to continue.

"We gave it a five-year run but, yeah, a few
years ago we finally called it quits."

"And now she's married to your brother,"
Shandie said. "Does that bother you?"

Another shrug.

"It's just weird, isn't it? I mean, she was
my wife, he's my brother—weird."

"But do you *care?*" Okay, so she was digging because she suddenly—and for no rea-

son she was comfortable exploring—wanted badly to know that he didn't still have feelings for his ex.

Dax seemed to consider that question before he said, "No, I don't really *care*—I don't feel jealous or as if I can't stand the thought of them being together or anything. It just strikes me as strange—my former wife is now my sister-in-law. If they have kids, my ex-wife's kids will be my nieces and nephews. I'm sure I'll get used to the idea, but you have to admit, it's strange."

Shandie hesitated, but then decided she couldn't keep her thought to herself. "Is that contributing to this sort of life crisis you're in? Did having your brother get together with your ex-wife make you feel like maybe you made a mistake letting her go?"

Dax's head pivoted on his hands to cast her a knowing—and smug—smile. "I don't want Allaire back," he said decisively. "She's a decent person but I told you, if we hadn't rushed into things I doubt the marriage ever would have happened at all. And I do hope it works out for them. Hell, if anything, D.J. has earned that just from waiting for her as long as he did. And to be honest, they're more suited to each other than Allaire and I ever were."

Shandie studied him for a moment, searching for signs that he was speaking from pride rather than truth. But there was no indication of that, and she finally decided that she believed him.

"After Allaire, was there anyone you were serious about? Until Lizbeth Stanton?"

Dax made yet another face, and Shandie couldn't decipher this one. There were hints of confusion in it, but more that she just couldn't figure out. Self-disgust, maybe?

"Lizbeth Stanton," he repeated. "No, there was no one I was serious about between Allaire and Lizbeth. And with Lizbeth...*that* was just craziness."

"How so?"

He frowned up at the ceiling. "It was craziness in just about every way it could have been. I met her when she was tending bar at the resort. She was new to town, and I'd see her here and there, and at the bar. I started hanging out at the bar more than I should have, escaping my own doldrums, I guess. We hit it off, started dating some, even though she's pretty young—at twenty-four she's six years younger than I am."

"Maybe that was part of the appeal—the sweet young thing?" Shandie said, teasing him but fishing, too.

"Nah, that wasn't it."

"What was *it?*"

He shrugged without taking his hands from behind his head. "She had a lot of…enthusiasm for life, I suppose you could say. And I just sort of clamped on to her coattails and hoped all that energy and bubbliness would carry me out of the pits."

"It didn't, though?"

"When I was with her it seemed—at least on the surface—as if things were picking up for me. I didn't really feel any better, I wasn't any happier with my life and the way things have played out, but she was the first relationship I'd had in a while and it *looked* as if I was finally getting myself on track. Then D.J. and Allaire got engaged and I thought, *Hey, why not go the whole nine yards…"*

"You asked her to marry you because of your brother and your ex-wife?"

"It wasn't a jealousy thing. Or an I'll-show-you thing." He was quick to read exactly what Shandie was thinking. "It was more that D.J. and Allaire getting together, getting engaged, was just another example of how everyone else was moving forward. And I figured maybe I should take that step, too. That if I acted like things were okay, they might actually start being okay. Nothing else had worked, so why not try that, you know? That's what was going through my head."

"And was it your plan to *act* as if things were okay with just whoever was in range at the time? Or were you genuinely in love with Lizbeth Stanton?"

"I liked her all right," Dax said defensively. "I wasn't using her or anything—the way you make that sound. But, well, to tell you the truth, we really were strangers. I mean, I may not have known Allaire deep down, but I *knew* her. With Lizbeth? It was all just on the surface. The whole time we were together I didn't talk to her the way you and I have talked already. I didn't know as much about her as I know about you now."

"And yet she accepted the proposal?" Shandie asked.

Dax pulled his hands out from behind his head and sat up straight, angling to face her and stretching an arm along the back of the sofa. "I'm a persuasive guy," he said with a sly and very engaging grin. Then he went on. "Lizbeth hadn't made any secret of the fact that she saw marriage in her future, that that was what she ultimately wanted. Not that she was angling for it with me, just in general. But when—for my own crazy reasons—it seemed like a good idea, I popped the question and yeah, she said yes."

"But you didn't get to the altar this time," she prompted.

"No. I knew right away that I wasn't in it for the right reasons, and before I ended up with *two* divorces to my name, I broke it off. Now Lizbeth is hooked up with Mitch Cates, and he's probably a whole lot better for her."

"You seem to think both of your exes are better off without you," Shandie observed.

"When it's not right, it's not right."

"Any lingering regrets about the breakup with Lizbeth Stanton?"

"Not that we broke up, no. I wasn't the one for her, she wasn't the one for me. It was just a lapse of sanity that—luckily—didn't go too far."

But it sounded as if he regretted something. "Was she hurt?" Shandie asked.

Dax wasn't so quick to answer that. "There were some hard feelings, I think. We were both embarrassed, of course, since—like a jerk—I went and announced to everybody that we were getting married. So there were questions about why we weren't, what had happened—you know how that goes. It was uncomfortable for a while and Lizbeth seemed to take the breakup personally—"

"I guess so!" Shandie said. "How could she *not* take it personally?"

"Yeah, I know. But she shouldn't have. It wasn't as if I called it off because of something she did or something I learned about her or because I started to hate her."

"Did you make that clear when you called off the engagement?"

He looked slightly shamefaced. "I didn't really give her any reason for it—probably a lousy thing—"

"Probably? Definitely. How could you call off an engagement and not even tell her why?"

"Because the whole thing was just a dumb, impulsive, spur-of-the-moment deal that my own messed-up head made me think for a minute might be a solution. I didn't want to say that. Or that when I thought twice about it, I realized that it was a disaster in the making. Especially since neither one of us was really in love with the other one."

"You just didn't say anything?"

Dax's grimace showed his regret. "I know, it was a rotten way to handle it. But it's not as if I've been on a roll lately with how I've handled anything."

"Are you sure she *wasn't* in love with you?"

"Oh, yeah," he said without hesitation. Then he amended it to, "Well, I'm pretty sure she had feelings for me, but no, I don't believe she was in love with me. It was more… Have you ever been in one of those arcade machines that simulate driving, or car or motorcycle racing? I think what we were both playing at was that—a simulation of the real thing because we both wished it was the real thing. But it just wasn't."

"So, with Allaire, you think that was puppy love taken too far, and with Lizbeth you think it was just a simulation of love. Doesn't that mean that you haven't *ever* felt the real thing, then?"

"I never thought of it like that. But…yeah, you might be right." He smiled that irresistibly wicked grin again and raised only a finger from the cushion behind her to smooth her hair away from her face. "I could just be a babe in the woods when it comes to the real thing."

Shandie laughed but the simple touch of

that finger had already had enough effect on her to make it a throaty, seductive sound. "Somehow I doubt you're a babe in the woods when it comes to much of anything."

"Oh, good, you've noticed," he joked in a low, intimate voice before he leaned forward and kissed her.

It was strange how the past few days seemed like nothing but time she filled until she could be with him again.

She knew that was likely something she should be paying attention to, maybe analyzing and taking as a warning because the rest of her life shouldn't have been merely what she got through to get her back to this. But at that moment she just couldn't have cared less. All she could do was what she was doing— revel in that kiss she was returning with lips parted and breath mingling and a hand of her own that was already flat against the solid wall of his chest, her fingers pulsing into him.

His mouth opened wider and Shandie followed his lead, freeing the way for his tongue to come boldly to greet hers as he brought the hand from the sofa to cradle her head and wrapped his other arm around her.

He was certainly no babe in the woods when it came to plundering her mouth. But

Shandie held her own, eager to keep pace, to learn every game and play it to the hilt.

Her other hand rose to the side of his strong, thick neck, then coiled around to his nape and down to the expanse of his broad shoulders.

She wasn't sure whether he pulled her closer or she pulled him, but closer they were, with her front nesting against his.

She slid the hand at his chest to his side to get it out of the way of her breasts, her nipples high and hard. Could he feel just how hard they were through their clothes?

Possibly, because both of his hands were suddenly on her sides, their heels pressing her breasts from there, pulling them tighter to him.

It only made her nipples all the more insistent and when she didn't deny him that much, Dax located her sweater's hem and nudged underneath it.

His hands were hot on her skin and every bit a man's hands—big, slightly rough, but taking care to be gentle as one remained low on her spine and the other retraced the route to the edge of her breast.

Mouths were wide, tongues were toying erotically by then, and the anticipation of having his hand fully on her breast caused Shandie to writhe just a little with the ever-growing yen for him to finally reach her, touch her, show her what he could do with his mechanic's grasp.

A small, almost guttural sound came from deep in his throat just before he did exactly that, covering her breast with a hand that nearly dwarfed it.

Oh, if only she hadn't worn a bra!

Even the thin lace of it was too much barrier between that taut, straining nipple and his touch.

Then that hand on her spine sluiced upward and in one easy motion, the bra was unhooked and she was free.

Under the cup he came, warm and tender, firm in his caress of her oh-so-sensitive flesh, his palm making the perfect cove for her nipple to kernel into before he began to massage, to knead, to tug and tease first the entire globe and then the nipple itself with fingers that knew just the right amount of force to use.

Circling, rolling, plucking that fragile crest, tonight he didn't merely awaken things inside of her that had been long sleeping, he electrified them.

Shandie had no idea when her own hands had gone under his sweater, but she was aware of the fact that they were filled with the smooth, calfskin-over-steel feel of his skin.

She kneaded his back, digging her fingers into him even as that hand at her back dropped to her rump to bring her closer to him before traipsing along the back of her thigh and uncurling her leg to position it around his hip.

She wasn't sure if what their mouths were doing could still be called kissing as they hungered for each other, as tongues thrust and threw off all restraint.

There was something untamed let loose in Shandie that she'd never known existed before and that leg he'd repositioned curved completely behind him, putting her nearly in his lap.

He flexed forward, inviting even more as his hand worked glories at her breast— going from one to the other so neither was neglected and both were alive with wanting even more from him. With nearly crying out for his mouth there instead.

Thinking of how much she wanted to be rid of her own top, Shandie raised her hands to his shoulders, taking his higher. High enough that he got the message and broke away from her mouth so she could pull his sweater off.

Then he was back again, his mouth ravaging hers, one hand turning the bud of her breast into a burgeoning blossom of yearning that caused her to strain for more, the other on her rear, his fingers digging into her while she savored the unfettered freedom and expanse of his naked, massively muscled upper half.

Then he brought that hand that was on her derriere to the back of her waistband instead, following the strip of denim around to the front where he unfastened the brass button...

Almost everything in her shouted, *Yes! Unzip them! Take them off! Let me feel you there, too!*

Almost everything.

But somewhere far in the back of her mind a small, quiet voice said, *Uh-oh...*

Should she really let this happen?

She wanted to.

She wanted to very, very badly.

But *should* she?

Oh-h-h-h...probably not.

And even though *probably* wasn't *definitely,* it was still enough for her to clamp her hand over his as he reached for her zipper and stop him.

He also stopped kissing her, looked at her from beneath eyebrows arched loftily on that achingly handsome face, and said, "No?"

"I don't think so. I don't know. But no. Maybe not."

He smiled a slightly distressed smile. "If it isn't an absolute, certified yes, then it's a no."

She couldn't give him an absolute, certified yes. She wanted to. But she just wasn't sure...

She shook her head and whispered, "Then for now, I think it has to be a no."

He nodded. But he kissed her again. A long, slow, sexy kiss that took her another notch nearer to yes before he ended it, gave her breast one final, lingering squeeze, then released it, too, and refastened her bra.

That bit of lace required some adjusting, but she seized the opportunity to do that when he retrieved his sweater from the floor in front of the sofa.

She also devoured the sight of his bare chest—a view that was no less than mouth-watering and set her to wondering if she'd made a mistake to stop when she was craving so much more of him again.

But she didn't act on that craving. Instead she refastened her jeans as if that put some irrevocable finality to it all.

Dax stood then and she did, too. Silently, they both went to the front door where he opened it as if he needed the cold blast of snow-laden air that came flooding inside.

"Thanks for letting me use your garage tonight," Shandie said, thinking that it sounded feeble at that point.

Dax merely nodded again, his dark, dark eyes on her as surely as his hands had been moments before.

He leaned forward and kissed her again with lips parted, soft and so, so tempting.

Then he stopped. Said nothing. And left.

And as Shandie watched him walk through the falling snow, all she wanted was for him to turn around and come back, whisk her upstairs to her downy bed and make love to her until she couldn't walk.

But she held her breath so she couldn't call to him, staying there in the frigid air even after he'd driven away.

And still she wasn't totally convinced that she shouldn't have just said yes after all....

Chapter Eight

"These-uz is all the bunch of new ormanents we buy'd," Kayla announced to Dax late Sunday evening.

Shandie considered the corrections she should have made in her daughter's sentence, but she decided against interjecting an English lesson into what was the end of a terrific day.

Sunday morning had dawned with the worst of recent weather predictions having come true—thirty-two inches of snow had fallen overnight. With no way for Shandie's sedan to get through it in order for her and Kayla to go buy a Christmas tree, Shandie had been in the middle of trying to console her distraught and disappointed three-year-old when Dax had come to the rescue. Kayla had talked and talked about their tree plans while Shandie had painted the preschool program clouds on Saturday night, so he'd been well aware of what they'd intended to do today. He'd also realized when he'd seen the snow that it wouldn't be possible to accomplish it. So he'd called and offered to take them on his snowmobile.

After the way the previous evening had ended—and the unsatisfied stirrings that had kept Shandie awake most of the night—there wasn't anything she'd wanted so much as to see him again. Wise or unwise. And because he was providing a solution to her problem, she'd accepted.

By the time he'd picked them up at two that afternoon he'd persuaded his friend, Russ Chilton, to let them cut down a tree off Russ's ranch property. Dax had also gone to his other friend—ranch and farm equipment supplier Mitch Cates—to borrow the necessary chain saw and ax. Topping it all off, Dax had procured a sled and rope to pull behind the snowmobile for dragging the tree back into town, and set everything into motion for Shandie and Kayla to have their first experience cutting down their own Christmas tree. Or, at least, picking one out and watching him do the work.

Shandie had had some concerns about taking Kayla on the snowmobile, but Dax had brought the little girl a helmet and guaranteed that he would keep his speed to a minimum. So, with Kayla firmly sandwiched in front of Shandie and behind Dax, Dax had taken them into the countryside and they'd had a full afternoon of tree cutting.

While Dax and Kayla had built a stand for the tree once they'd gotten it home, Shandie had made a quick supper for them all. After that they'd strung the tree with lights, then hung shiny multicolored glass balls, plastic candy canes and the decorations from previous years that Shandie had unpacked. And now they were down to the newest batch of ornaments Shandie and Kayla had picked out for this year—saving those for last.

"Or*m*-a-*n*ents, huh?" Dax repeated the little girl's mispronunciation as he sat on the couch beside the box of new purchases that Kayla was peering into.

"Uh-huh," Kayla confirmed. "I picked-ed 'em out. We gots Santa wis a cute puppy dog, and a snowman in a bucket," she said, describing them as she took them from the box and handed them to him. "Lookit, here's a mouse sittin' in a cupcake. An' this one's a kitty peekin' outta a present. An' here's a pitty pincess what looks like me."

"Yes, she does," Dax agreed.

"We still have the angel to put on top of the tree, too," Shandie reminded them from where she was draping strands of tinsel carefully over the branches. "And it's past your bedtime, Miss Kayla Jane, so let's get to it."

"We gots to puts hooks on 'em," Kayla said. "An' here's the wa'rus, too!" she added when she discovered one last ornament.

Shandie had looked away from the scene on the sofa, but when her daughter burst into giggles she glanced back.

"What?" Dax inquired innocently, as if he had no idea why the child was laughing. But he'd put hooks on two of the ornaments and hung them around the tops of his ears to dangle on his chiseled cheeks.

"You don' *wear* 'em!" Kayla told him amidst her nearly hysterical laughter.

"What're you talking about?" he asked, playing dumb.

Kayla looked to her mother. "Dax gots orm-a-nents in his ears. He's funny!"

"I think we should make him wear them in to work tomorrow," Shandie suggested.

Kayla laughed even harder. "Wis the big bikes—he'd be silly."

"Because he doesn't look silly now," Shandie goaded.

"We has to put 'em on the tree," Kayla said then, reaching without warning to yank the snowman free, surprising Dax and making him yelp.

Shandie couldn't help laughing at that, especially when Dax removed the second ornament in a hurry before her daughter had the chance.

"Guess you'll think twice about that the next time, won't you?" she said in an aside to him.

But Dax wasn't actually injured and merely uttered a "Yow!" as he rubbed his ear.

There were no hard feelings, though, as he finished applying hooks to the remainder of the new ornaments. Then he and Kayla brought them to the tree to find places for them.

Since he seemed to be enjoying the decorating as much as Kayla was, Shandie went on stringing tinsel and left them to that.

"When're you gonna put up yur tree?" Kayla asked him as they did.

"I don't usually put up a tree," Dax told her.

"Why?" Kayla exclaimed with horror.

"I don't have any ormanents," he said.

"You could buy some," the little girl reasoned.

"I could," he allowed just as they finished the last of the new decorations, too. Then he changed the subject by pointing to the angel tree topper. "How about you get on my shoulders like we did at the parade, I'll climb on the ladder, and you can put the angel on top?"

"I don't know about the logistics of that," Shandie contributed. "Maybe you better just let Dax do it because he's the tallest."

"We'll be fine," he assured, orchestrating Kayla climbing to the back of the couch while he sat on the arm so she could get on his shoulders. Then he did as he'd said he would and climbed the few steps on Shandie's kitchen step stool until Kayla was within range.

"Hang on," Shandie warned, fearing they were both going to tumble into the tree.

But they didn't and Kayla managed to get the angel onto the tree's top branch—askew, but up there nonetheless.

Then Dax took her back to the sofa, squatted low enough to safely dump the little girl backward onto the soft cushions and make her laugh again.

Without a word, he went into the entryway to where his fleece-lined suede coat was hanging on the hall tree and returned with a small, gaily wrapped package in his hand. Bringing it to Kayla, he held it out to her and said, "Here you go—your first Christmas present this year."

Shandie had finished with the tinsel and went to the sofa to see what was going on.

"Can I open it?" her daughter asked her.

"That's up to Dax. He gave it to you."

"You better open it or it'll go to waste," he advised.

Kayla didn't hesitate to rip the wrapping to shreds to find a Christmas tree–shaped night-light inside.

"I saw it at the gas station when I went to fill the snowmobile's tank and I thought this way you could have a tree of your own in your room," he explained.

"Can I put ormanents on it?"

"When we plug it in it'll look like it has lights and ornaments on it already," Shandie informed her. "What do you say to Dax?"

"Thank yoo-oo," Kayla complied as she

hopped down from the couch. "Le's go plug it in!"

Shandie glanced at Dax. "Good timing," she said in another aside before addressing her daughter. "We'll plug it in as soon as I get you into your pajamas and you go to bed, which you need to do right now."

With the lure of the new night-light the child didn't put up a fuss, running for the stairs with her treasure.

"Tell Dax thanks for everything today, too, and say good-night," Shandie called after her.

Kayla repeated her mother's words by rote and climbed the steps.

"We still need work on the delivery," Shandie said to excuse her daughter's less-than-heartfelt recitation.

"It's okay. I know she had a good time today."

"She did," Shandie answered.

Dax cast a glance toward the front door then, as if she'd given him a cue that it was time to end the evening.

Or was he just thinking about it himself?

There was no doubt it would be better if he left. Safer. It would remove temptation from her path.

But she didn't want him to go. Not yet. They hadn't had any time to themselves.

He didn't say anything about going, though.

And neither did Shandie.

Instead she said, "This will only take a few minutes."

"Don't rush. There's no hurry," he countered.

And for some reason, she wondered if he was only referring to her putting Kayla to bed, or if he was also telling her there was no hurry on that other front that had begun the night before, too. That she shouldn't feel pressured.

But she didn't feel pressured. Inclined, maybe. But not pressured...

"When I come back we can sit by the fire and look at the tree," she suggested.

"I'd like that," he said.

Shandie followed in Kayla's wake then, but once she was on the third step she paused to look back into the living room. Dax was picking up some of the debris and wasn't aware that she hadn't gone all the way upstairs yet.

He looked as good as always in a pair of jeans and a black turtleneck sweater that hugged that torso she'd gotten to see bare the night before, only adding to its grandeur.

And the ripple of appreciation for the sight of him let her know that what had come alive in her on Saturday night wasn't too far below the surface tonight.

Making that temptation he'd left in her path all the greater....

It took Shandie about twenty minutes to get Kayla to bed and then she made a quick pit stop in the bathroom. As she washed her hands, she took stock of herself in the mirror behind the sink.

When they'd returned to the house with the Christmas tree she'd changed out of the snow-crusted jeans and heavy sweatshirt she'd worn against the cold, and put on another pair of jeans and a baby-blue velvet hoodie that zipped up the front. She'd left her hair in the clip at the back of her head to keep it contained, though, and she decided on the spur of the moment now to unclip it and brush it to fall around her face instead.

Mascara and blush had been refreshed earlier and didn't need another retouch, but she did apply a coat of lip gloss.

Then she did one more thing.

She lowered the zipper on her hoodie.

Not a lot. Just about an inch. Probably not

enough for Dax to even notice, and all the while telling herself that since she would be sitting when she got to the living room again the hoodie could pull back and be tight around her throat if she didn't give herself some leeway.

But the tiny flutter of sensual longing deep in the pit of her stomach let her know comfort wasn't the only issue.

She didn't raise the zipper again, however. She merely went out of the bathroom and back down the stairs.

The sound of the vacuum cleaner greeted her as she neared the bottom step. Sure enough, when she looked from there into the other room Dax was running it. She'd taken it out to vacuum up pine needles once the tree was up and had not put it away because she'd known there would be more cleaning necessary when the tree was finished. But she hadn't intended that to be a hint for Dax to do the job.

Still, there he was, one hand on the upright's handle, his other hand slung in his pocket, the cord draped over his shoulder—the man was cool even when playing housemaid. And so attractive it nearly made her heart skip a beat.

Seeing him like that also inspired a smile as she paused to watch him perform the everyday household chore.

They'd all taken off their shoes when they'd gotten home so, like Shandie, he was in his stocking feet, and he presented an odd combination of renegade and domesticity that was endearing and sexy at once.

He caught sight of her as he flipped off the vacuum, and Shandie had to stop staring and go the rest of the distance into the living room.

"You didn't have to do that," she told him as she did. "Or any of the rest of this," she added when she realized that he'd neatly stacked all the empty boxes and packaging remnants in one corner of the room so it was almost as neat as it had been before they'd begun today.

"Now we can sit back and relax," he said, winding up the vacuum's cord.

Then he relinquished the machine to her so she could put it in the hall closet.

When she got back to the living room he'd taken the quilt she kept draped over the cracked headrest of an antique rocking chair and he was spreading it on the floor in front of the rustic redbrick fireplace. Then he sat leaning against the hearth, one leg curved in front of him, the other bent at the knee to casually brace a forearm while he patted the blanket beside him in invitation to her. "The best seat in the house," he said, referring to the front-row view of the Christmas tree.

Shandie went first to the lamp on the end table beside the sofa, turning it off so that the Christmas lights were the only illumination. Then she situated herself next to him on the blanket, sitting cross-legged.

"Now squint your eyes at the tree," she commanded. "It'll be all blurry and sparkling."

He laughed at her indulgently, much as he had done numerous times today with her daughter. But he did it, screwing up his face to accomplish the squint.

"See how pretty it is?" she said, squinting herself once she was sure he was following orders.

"I see a couple of sections that could use more lights," he said conversely.

"Still pretty," she judged.

"Mmm," he agreed with a lascivious intonation before she opened her eyes and saw that he'd gone from studying the tree to studying her.

Shandie opted to ignore the flattery—despite the fact that it pleased her—and move on.

"Thanks for all of this today," she said. "Kayla isn't the only one who had a good time, and you made the beginning of our first Christmas in Thunder Canyon something to remember."

"Glad to be of service," he said with a lazy smile. "I had a good time, too. It's been forever since I did any Christmas tree cutting."

"We both loved the snowmobile, too."

"You've really never been on one before?"

"Never."

"Any time you want to do it again, there are all kinds of trails I can take you on—some that the resort uses as hiking trails in the summer and some others that are more off the beaten track, leading up into higher ground that's good for overland skiing or just watching the herds of deer and elk."

"Sounds like you know the countryside pretty well," Shandie observed.

"Sure. As kids, D.J. and the Cates brothers, and Grant and Russ and I all spent time scoping it out. We skied, hiked, camped, hunted, fished. Plus, I used to like to take my motorcycle off-road, go out on my own sometimes. I know it all like the back of my hand."

"Hmm," Shandie mused as the wheels of her mind began to turn in problem-solving mode.

"*Hmm* what?" he inquired.

"I was just thinking that it seems like there could be a whole lot more your business could offer if you branched out into that."

He gave her the confused frown she'd become familiar with. "If I branched out into what?"

"Well, why couldn't you sell snowmobiles and off-road and all-terrain vehicle kind of things along with motorcycles? And repair them, too. Are they something else you can fix?"

"Sure, I can fix about anything with a motor or an engine. But I'm not doing a bang-up business as it is. Expanding seems like something you do when things are booming, not when you're on the verge of busting. I'm also not sure how big the market around here is for that other stuff, either."

"What if you created the market?"

He looked at her as if she were out of her mind. "How would I do that?"

"Even though your shop isn't booming,

Thunder Canyon is—thanks to the resort—right?"

"Right."

"Couldn't you do something in connection with that—like convince the resort to buy snowmobiles or those other ATV things from you? They could have them available to their guests and you could do any repairs and upkeep. Plus…" The wheels really were turning and something else occurred to her. "What if you even offered to take guests into the countryside, on the trails or out to snowshoe or ski the way you just offered to take me? You could be the guide to the backcountry, too."

He was smiling at her with a crinkled-up brow. And although the smile was slightly bemused, she could tell he was intrigued by what she was suggesting. "How would I expand my sales and my repairs *and* be the guide into the backcountry, too?"

"You could set aside only certain times—or certain days—to do tours, and hire someone to cover the shop when you weren't there."

He laughed. "Ah, now you even have me hiring help. You're just full of ideas, aren't you?"

"If Kayla and I liked doing what we did

today, why wouldn't other people? Summer and winter? The resort is looking to offer more and more to attract tourists—this would be another attraction, wouldn't it? And here you are, in a position to be in on the ground floor of it. It could be exciting. And take you from being on the verge of busting to booming along with everyone else."

"Just like that?" he said as if she were oversimplifying.

"Why not just like that? You even have an in with the resort's bigwigs—Grant Clifton manages it, and there's Riley Douglas. You're friends with him, too, aren't you?"

"Yes, but—"

"Couldn't you talk to Grant? I'll bet he'd jump at the chance to have this other outdoorsy activity to offer resort guests, and he'd probably go to bat for you with Riley Douglas. So why *not* just like that?" she repeated.

"I can think of half a dozen reasons— money for starters."

"There are always complications—like the construction on the remodel of the Clip 'n Curl taking so much longer than it was supposed to. But anything can be worked out. And if the resort commits to buying the snowmobiles and the ATVs before you invest anything, the money you'd be using would be theirs. You wouldn't even need a loan to get things going."

He smiled as if he liked what he was seeing in her. "Do you always have this much energy?"

"Most days."

"No wonder your cousin Judy asked you to be her partner in the beauty shop."

"She was talking about how business was hurting and why. I told her what I thought would help," Shandie confirmed matter-of-factly. "Like now, with you," she added. "For whatever it's worth."

He was staring at her, a sparkle of amusement lighting his eyes, and something else there, too. "I'll think about it," he said, seriously enough to let her know he honestly would.

But she also had the impression that he was saying he didn't want to talk about his business anymore, that he wanted to mull over expansion on his own, and that was verified when he changed the subject.

"So you're teeming with business ideas and plans for the future—for everybody—but what about for Shandie herself? What plans do you have for you alone?"

"You mean, like, personally?"

"Yeah, like personally," he said, taking her hand.

Shandie tried not to notice the little charge that skipped up her arm at his touch and said, "I don't really have plans. I guess I just go day to day."

"One day at a time—has that always been the case or just since your husband passed?"

"It's been since I got involved with Pete, really. He lived for the moment because he couldn't be sure how much future he had, and I guess I learned to do that, too."

"So, pretend you have to come up with a plan for yourself right now. What would it be? Would you outlaw marriage? Is Kayla enough of a family for you? Do you see a dog in your future…?" he finished as if a dog would be a much bigger change than anything he'd mentioned before it.

Shandie laughed as much at that as at the feathery strokes of his thumb along the back of her wrist. "I don't know about a dog," she said as if she agreed that that was the weightier possibility.

"But marriage and more kids…" he reiterated.

He probably thought she was considering it when he let that dangle in the air and she still didn't answer him right away. But marrying again and having more kids were things she'd thought about a lot. What she was actually doing at that moment was marveling at the sudden realization that, for the first time since her husband's death, she could think about those two things without pain or guilt.

Which, she also realized, was true of what was going on with Dax, too. Because before this, even considering dating someone had filled her with both pain *and* guilt. And while she didn't know if what they were doing was dating, surprisingly she hadn't felt those with him.

"Yeah," she finally answered his question. "I suppose I could see myself getting married again and having maybe one or two more kids." Then, not wanting to dwell on it, she said, "What about you? I know you aren't against the idea of marrying again if you just jumped into an engagement to Lizbeth Stanton. But where do you stand on kids?"

He grinned. "I try not to stand on them. They yell a lot if I do."

"Bad joke," she decreed, laughing anyway.

"I'd like to have kids," he answered then, seriously. "I didn't want them when I was married to Allaire, mainly because we were young and having kids seemed like a drag— something that would tie us down too much. But now...why not? Especially if I end up a motorcycle-ATV-snowmobile mogul."

"Oh, especially then," she said, playing along with his teasing her about her idea.

He apparently appreciated that she had because he grinned at her. "You're a good sport, you know?"

"Just what every girl wants to be—a good sport," she said, rolling her eyes.

"Better than being a bad sport."

"But not as good as being the bodacious bombshell babe from Bootyland."

He laughed—a hearty, barrel-chested laugh that she loved.

"You did not just say bodacious bombshell babe from Bootyland," he said.

"I didn't?"

He closed the grip on her hand and pulled her to sit in front of him, close enough that she was leaning back against him. "Just look at the lights," he said as if her comment had cost her the privilege of conversation.

She didn't mind. How could she when it was so nice to be sitting in the V of his widespread legs, his shoulder her headrest, his arms coming around to encircle her?

And as they sat there with the only illumination coming from the fire and the Christmas lights, the only sound the crackle of the flames, Shandie thought again about what had just come to her moments before—the fact that she hadn't felt any guilt about being with Dax. About how everything with him had just evolved so naturally that it had never seemed as if she were cheating on Pete or being unfaithful to his memory.

She wasn't sure if the passage of time had made it possible, or if it only had to do with Dax, but it left her feeling that she was in a good place suddenly. In Thunder Canyon. In this house. In her life. In this man's arms.

And while she reminded herself that Dax might not be a *forever-friend*—or someone who she was likely to have a future with—and that she needed to keep her eyes open when it came to him, the fact that he was a part of reaching this good place now made it feel okay to be there with him. To have kissed him. To have more than kissed him the night before. To want that next step with him, and maybe to have it if she just didn't expect it to be anything serious...

He dipped his head so his face was close to the side of hers and, in a quiet, husky voice, said, "Are you squinting?"

She tipped her head so she could look at him. "At the lights? No, are you?"

"Sorry," he said without contrition but with only a hint of a smile that was pure bad boy and that just plain turned her on.

That was when she knew she was going to give in to what she wanted to do, what she'd wanted to do the previous evening and every minute since then.

Somehow he seemed to register her decision because his hint of a smile stretched into a full, sexy, lopsided grin just before he nuzzled his way to her neck to kiss it, and pulled the cocoon of his arms tight enough around her to press his forearms into her breasts.

Her nipples instantly became pearls, and Shandie tilted her head farther still to give him more access as his tongue tickled the side of her neck and he sucked just enough to entice without leaving a mark.

She could feel him already beginning to harden where the juncture of his legs cradled her hip, and she couldn't suppress a smile of her own at the proof that he wanted her as much as she wanted him.

She raised a hand to his face, feeling the faint trace of roughness that his reemerging beard caused, and liking that sign of his masculinity, too.

"What about Kayla?" he whispered.

"She's sound asleep and her door is shut tight. It creaks like crazy when it opens so if she gets up for any reason there will be a lot of warning."

Dax nodded.

He kissed a line to her ear and nibbled the lobe for a moment before one of his hands came to tilt her chin so he could take her mouth with his.

Shandie made it easier and swiveled enough to almost face him, enough that she could respond to his kiss with equal devotion.

No finesse was needed for lips to part, for their kisses to be instantly sensual, for tongues to come together and part, circle and spar and mingle decadently.

She sent her hand around to his nape, testing the bristles of his hair there as one of his hands made the opposite journey, traveling downward from where it caressed her face to trail to where he'd left off Saturday night, clasping her breast—but only on the outside of her velvet top.

He wasn't wasting any time. Not that Shandie objected because it almost seemed as if her breasts hadn't stopped being aroused during the past twenty-four hours, and having his hand there again was welcome relief.

Mouths opened wider still and their kiss became so intense it pushed Shandie to rest against the inner side of Dax's upraised leg. Her head was braced by his knee as he ravaged and plundered with an abandon she met and matched.

Both of her arms were around him by then, her fingers digging into the thick cable knit of his sweater. She could feel the heat of him seeping through it and, added to the heat of the fire and what they were generating themselves, that seemed like a prime excuse to give herself what she'd been fantasizing about since first having it last night.

She found the hem of his sweater, escaped his kiss in order to pull it off over his head, and then reclaimed her place as her hands sought out the skin of that broad, bare back and the shoulders that were a shame to ever conceal.

His hand went to the zipper of her hoodie

then, inching it open and allowing her to burgeon from it in the filmy lace half-cup bra that gave away what had been on her mind even this morning when she'd first gotten out of the shower and chosen her underwear. It was sexier than having nothing on at all and, as if Dax could sense that there was something to see—or maybe just because he wanted to look—he took a turn at cutting off their kiss to have a peek.

A bold peek because as he pulled the hoodie off completely he devoured the sight of her breasts only scantily concealed by the bra, the shadow of her nipples visible through the lace.

He made a sound—a sort of gravelly sigh of awe and admiration just before he buried his face between her breasts. Then he took hold of the scalloped edge of one cup and pulled it low enough for flesh to bob above it and be caught by that mouth that had been on hers only moments earlier.

She might have missed the kissing except that what he was doing to her breast was too glorious not to make her close her eyes and breathe a sigh of her own.

Oh, what the man could do with tongue and teeth and the wet wonders of that mouth! He knew exactly the right amount of suction, of pressure and coercion, of hold and release. He knew the perfect combination of tugging and teasing, of firm and feathery, of flicking and tracing and tormenting until what he was setting alight in her was so bright and hot and demanding it made her gasp.

He unhooked her bra and tossed it aside, showing her other breast the wonders he'd introduced to the first. And even as he did, he laid her on the quilt, coming with her to lie beside and half on top of her. His mouth continued its marvels while his hand roamed from a farewell fondling of her free breast down her side to her waist and then forward to her stomach.

The tip of his index finger rolled an imaginary ball around the rim of her belly button and then dipped to the waistband of her low-ride jeans. He unfastened them. He unzipped them, too. But just when she thought he would dive inside—just when she *wanted* him to—he didn't.

Instead he coursed his palm and the heel of his hand on the outside of her jeans to cup her, pressing fingers to that spot that definitely didn't want the barrier of denim as interference.

It occurred to her then that denim was interfering on another front, too, and she suddenly wanted to be rid of it there as well. So she let her own hands go from their exploration of his amazing torso and his own taut male nibs, down his flat belly to the waistband of his jeans.

There was far more pressure coming to bear from inside his than hers. The waistband button popped easily and the zipper nearly opened itself.

What remained of their clothes came off rapidly then—but not before Dax took protection from his jeans pocket.

And there they were, together again on the quilt in front of the fire, naked body to naked body.

He kissed her once more, his mouth soft, supple, so, so sexy as his hand worked at her breast and one heavy thigh came over hers to rise between her legs.

Shandie could feel the long steely shaft of him against her side and she slipped her hand between them until she could close it around him.

He moaned a guttural moan that let her know just how glad he was to have her there as she learned the full length and breadth of the man while he slid his own hand from her breast, down her stomach and took that same dip he'd taken on the outside of her jeans before, this time without anything standing between them.

The small of her back rose off the quilt when he first touched her, when that initial finger slid inside. There was no controlling anything then—she wanted him, she needed him, and she couldn't have hidden it even if she'd tried.

But she didn't try. She opened her legs in invitation and after he'd quickly sheathed himself he raised above her, positioning himself where only his thigh had been before.

His hands were on the floor near her ears, elbows locked to hold his upper half high. Yet still he dropped his head to retake her mouth with his as his lower half came to her. Slowly and with care he entered her in one lithe, smooth sweep until she was filled with the grandeur that was Dax.

His tongue gave her a sneak preview, jutting into her mouth and out again. Then he lowered himself enough to draw her breast into that same moist, honeyed cave, pulling in her engorged flesh and letting his tongue make light, quick strikes to her nipple before he arched his back and pushed his hips completely into her, sealing them together.

She tightened her muscles around him and savored the feel of his big body over her, in her, as he began the ride that every ounce of her was screaming for. In and out, oh so slowly.

Then not so slowly.

Then so rapidly that she could only cling to him as he built in her a crystalline mountain of ever-increasing need. A mountain that he was helping her to climb, taking her higher and higher to where the air was so thin she could hardly breathe, to where she didn't need to breathe, to where there was only the two of them, their bodies one, striving for that peak that seemed unreachable until she broke through to the highest point, to the summit.

She froze in the throes of an ecstasy more pristine, more intense, more forceful and exquisite than anything she'd ever experienced, able only to hang on to him as he reached that same moment when everything exploded, when he, too, could only stay fixed in place and let his climax wash over him, through him, and carry them both to the other side.

Until the descent was all that was left...

Dax let out a thick, replete sigh.

Shandie became aware of the rise and fall of her breasts as she began to breathe again.

Dax's elbows buckled. He eased himself down to her, pulsing within her as if he'd found his home. He pressed a gentle kiss to the top of her shoulder, and she just let herself indulge for that moment in the wonderful sensation of their bodies fitted together so flawlessly.

Only after a while did he raise up again to look at her, to kiss her a long, lingering, sweet kiss before he slipped out of her and rolled to lie on his back. But even then he brought her with him to curve against his side and use his chest as a pillow.

"Wow," he whispered.

Shandie smiled against him. "Wow," she agreed in a whisper of her own.

Neither of them said anything else. They merely lay in each other's arms, legs entwined, her hand on his chest, his hand massaging the lowest curve of her back.

They stayed that way for a very long time. Dozing off and on. Shandie was lost in the primal feel of flesh to flesh, both of them wrapped in the quilt, warmed by the fire, dusted with the multicolored glow of Christmas lights.

Until real sleep was becoming unavoidable.

Then Dax kissed the top of her head and in a raspy voice said, "I'd like to be, but I don't think I *should* be here when Kayla gets up."

"No, probably not," Shandie agreed.

"I hate to go, though," he said, his tone so filled with regret she knew he meant it.

"I hate for you to go, too."

Still, neither of them moved. Or said anything else for another long while.

But then Dax sighed resignedly, hugged Shandie tight and kissed her—a deep, profound kiss.

"I'm gonna go," he told her when he'd ended it. "I don't want you to get up yet or walk me to the door because if you do, I won't be able to make myself leave. So wait, okay?"

"Okay," she agreed again, understanding because it was just too, too tempting to take him upstairs to her bed instead and worry about the morning when morning came.

He kissed her once again, another even deeper kiss that came very close to starting things all over.

But before he let that happen, he got up, covering her with the quilt before he stood.

It was divine torture to watch him dress in the firelight. To see that incredible, muscular male body in all its glory being stolen from her sight as he pulled on each article of clothing.

When he was finished, he knelt down beside her and she drank in what she knew was her last look at him that night—his tight sweater hugging his torso, the turtleneck brushing his chiseled jawline, his hair rumpled and roguish—and she just wanted to pull him back under the quilt and undress him again.

"I'll see you tomorrow," he said, bending to kiss her one last time.

"Okay," she responded, watching him get to his feet again.

Then he leaned down once more, stroked her hair, whispered, "Good night," and left.

And as she stayed there wrapped in the quilt, listening to the sounds of him leaving, she told herself that it was better that he hadn't spent the night. That they hadn't gone up to her bed. That he wouldn't be here in the morning.

And not only for the sake of Kayla.

It was also better because even at that moment Shandie had to fight to keep in mind that whatever this was between them, it wasn't a serious thing.

It couldn't be.

But keeping that in mind *was* a struggle.

Because in her heart of hearts, it seemed like more than that.

Chapter Nine

Monday was yet another day when not a single customer darkened the door of Dax's shop. But unlike every other day, he hadn't spent the time feeling sorry for himself.

And the sole reason for that was Shandie.

Making love with her the night before had rocked his world. In more ways than one. The lovemaking itself had been like nothing that had come before it, and it had done something to him that he couldn't fully comprehend. Something that had left him in a whole new frame of mind. And in that new frame of mind, not only were his empty hours filled with thoughts of her, they were also filled with thoughts about the things Shandie had said, including what she'd said about diversifying his business.

As a result, at three o'clock that afternoon, he closed up for the day and went to the resort to see Grant Clifton.

But now it was after four, and he and Grant were sitting at a table in the resort's lush Western-style lounge. They were nursing coffee, Dax had laid out the idea of supplying snowmobiles and ATVs to the resort and acting as guide to lead resort guests on excursions into the mountains on them. But rather than responding to it, Grant was simply staring at him, leaving Dax unsure how great the idea was after all.

"Look, it's okay if you don't think this will fly or you don't think Russ will want to invest in it right now or you guys don't want to do business with a friend," he said to give Grant an excuse, hiding his own disappointment. "I won't take offense. It was just a thought I wanted to run by you."

"No, it isn't any of that," Grant said, shaking his head, looking a little wide-eyed. "It's that I can't believe what I'm seeing and hearing here."

"Geez, I didn't think it was *that* over the top."

"The idea? The idea is great. It's what we're looking for on a couple of different levels. The resort already has four snowmobiles, but they're old models that need to be replaced. Some of the brochures advertise snowmobiling, but when there's interest in it we have to discourage it because there's too much liability in letting guests just go off alone on them into the high country. But you know the ins and outs of everything up here—how to avoid avalanche dangers, how not to get lost, how to do repairs if something should break down in the middle of nowhere. You're the perfect person to lead groups out, keep them safe, take care of anything that might happen."

Obviously Dax *had* garnered his friend's interest. He just hoped Grant wasn't letting him know it was a good idea before telling him why it couldn't happen. Or that Dax wasn't who would be included in it happening.

"And you know we'd be happy as all get-out to buy equipment through you and have you on the hook for upkeep," Grant continued. "Plus the ATV idea for the summer months?

We're desperate for things like that to get people in here off-season and that would be a great draw."

It didn't *seem* as if Grant was going to end with anything negative, but still Dax held his breath as his old friend went on.

"Besides taking tours out on the trails, you could get groups back into some of the more remote rivers and streams for fishing. And we could milk the romance elements, too—offer rustic mountain picnics or cookouts where you get the guests out to the best spots and we have one of the restaurants provide the food or a chef to do the cooking up there."

Dax couldn't stand wondering if he was being set up for a fall. "So you think it's feasible?" he said, cutting to the chase.

"I told you, it's a terrific idea. It's absolutely feasible."

"Why the stare, then?" Dax asked, still not understanding the reason behind his friend's looking at him as if he'd grown gills.

"I just…I can't believe *you*. Where's the hangdog Dax we've come to know and love lately? This is the old Dax—there's fire in your eyes again. You aren't sitting all slumped in the chair. Man, you're even smiling!"

"Hangdog? Have I been that bad?" Dax

asked with a laugh, not taking offense since what Grant had said before that made it seem as if he and the resort would accept the business proposition Dax had just presented.

"Yeah, you were that bad. Worse," Grant confirmed as if he suddenly felt free to not treat Dax as carefully as a glass with a crack in it. "Where'd this come from? What's happened to you all of a sudden?"

Dax shrugged. After the fiasco with Lizbeth he was reluctant to tell his old friend that a woman had inspired this. Grant might think it was on the order of his false-front happiness with Lizbeth.

"Maybe the time has come for me to get my act together," Dax said.

Grant studied him through narrowed eyes. "There's something else. And not like with Lizbeth when you were just going through the motions."

So Grant saw through him.

"Well, I feel different," Dax admitted to keep his friend from probing too deeply. "I guess I'm finally ready to quit sulking about things not working out the way I wanted them to, and get on with it."

"I can't tell you how good it is to hear that. To know you mean it this time—because I think you really do. But I still think there's something else going on with you."

For better or worse, at that moment D.J. came into the lounge. It distracted Grant from pursuing the subject of what had caused the change in Dax, but it was still D.J. And the sudden appearance of his brother was enough to put Dax on edge in spite of what seemed like a win for him on the career front.

Both Dax and Grant watched as D.J. headed for the burled oak bar and the bartender behind it. D.J. didn't glance at the tables, so he was unaware that Grant and Dax were sitting at one of them.

"How far does this new lease on life extend?" Grant asked Dax as D.J. began to talk to the bartender.

Dax knew Grant was referring to the strained relationship between D.J. and Dax.

But Dax didn't have a ready answer for his friend. Instead, that one glimpse of his brother made everything Shandie had said on the subject of his problems with D.J. flash through his mind. She'd been right about expanding his business. Was she right about his brother, too?

For a moment Dax gave that some thought. Did he *want* things to go on the way they were with D.J.? Shandie wasn't the only one to point out recently that he and D.J. were all that was left of their immediate family now. They'd never been close, but if things weren't put together somehow—soon—he knew they never would be. That brothers or not, they were going to end up enemies.

And he knew he *didn't* want that.

"Yeah, I should probably have a sit-down with him," Dax muttered, more to himself than to Grant, still watching his brother discuss something with the bartender.

"Go for it," Grant suggested.

Dax continued to stare at his brother, debating whether or not to take that step, too, today.

Maybe it was the high he was still feeling over last night with Shandie. Maybe it was the additional high of Grant's reaction to the snowmobile/ATV idea, but now actually didn't seem like a bad time to bury the hatchet....

"D.J.," he heard himself call across the lounge to get his brother's attention.

D.J. glanced up at the sound of his name, searching for the origin. Since happy hour was only just beginning it didn't take much for him to spot Dax and Grant.

The frown that came to D.J.'s face the minute he saw Dax didn't bode well for a warm family reunion, but when Grant motioned for D.J. to come to the table, D.J. ended his conversation with the bartender and headed in their direction.

"My liquor order was short this morning. I wondered if it was delivered in here instead," D.J. said to Grant as he reached the table, apparently believing it had been Grant who had called his name. Then he turned his gaze to his brother. "Dax," he said with reservation.

"Can you spare a few minutes?" Dax asked.

D.J.'s expression showed surprise. But it also gave evidence of suspicion and reluctance to comply.

"We're getting ready for the dinner crowd, I should be at The Shack," he said.

"Come on, sit," Grant urged.

D.J. looked from Dax to Grant and then back again. And still Dax could tell his younger brother was inclined to leave.

But then he must have reconsidered because he said, "I suppose everything will get done without me there for a while."

D.J. sat down, but he was stiff and wary. And he didn't say anything.

But since Dax had initiated this, he knew it was up to him to take it from there.

"I've been doing a lot of thinking," he said. "I know not long ago you told me you thought it was time we talked, and when that didn't happen... Well, nothing's changed between us. And I agree, it needs to. Like you said then—and other people have said, too—we are all that's left of the family, and I don't want things to stay the way they are."

D.J.'s eyebrows rose. But all he said was, "Yeah?"

Their waitress came to the table then to tell Grant he was needed at the front desk. Grant tried to put her off, but she insisted she'd been told it was important, that there was a problem with a guest that had to be addressed immediately.

Still Grant didn't rush to go even after the waitress left. He eyed Dax and D.J. "If I leave, are you two going to tear up the place—and each other?"

"No," Dax answered him.

"D.J.?" Grant said.

"We'll be fine," D.J. answered but with his gaze locked on Dax.

"Honest, it's okay," Dax insisted. "I'm gonna do whatever it takes to make this right."

Shock was evident on the faces of both other men, but Grant finally conceded to the demands on him and stood.

As if that might have been enough to set them off, he paused to watch them another moment.

Then he said, "Behave yourselves," and finally followed in the waitress's wake.

Alone together, D.J. repeated Dax's words. "You're going to do whatever it takes to make this right?"

Dax had been sitting with is forearms on the table, and now he sat back in his chair, keeping his eyes steady on his brother. "I am," he said without the slightest challenge or chip on his shoulder for once.

D.J.'s only response was to stare at him.

"Someone, someone pretty smart," Dax began, "has recently opened my eyes to some things. About me and about you, too. And here's how it is. Since the accident my life has seemed to me to be going downhill. Which is bad enough, but at the same time everybody else's life has been going uphill. And even though I really am happy for everybody, I've felt like the odd man out—"

"You?" D.J. said as if he couldn't believe it.

"Yeah, me. How could I not have felt that

way when I've been watching everybody succeed and hook up with who they're meant to be hooked up with, while I've been failing at business and at relationships? What that means is that I haven't fit in with you all. And it's been lousy," Dax concluded with force.

"It's lousy all right," D.J. agreed sardonically.

But for the first time, Dax thought he understood what was behind his brother's attitude and he told him so. "You know firsthand how lousy it is," he said. "That's what my eyes were opened to about you, that that was how you must have felt at home, growing up—like the odd man out."

D.J. reared back slightly in shock but didn't confirm or deny Dax's statement.

"It *is* how you felt, isn't it?" Dax persisted.

D.J. shrugged but that seemed to be as far as he was willing to go in the way of concession.

"It's how you have to have felt," Dax said. "You and me and Dad—after Mom died and there was just the three of us. It should have *been* the three of us. But instead it was Dad and me doing the motorcycle thing and you basically on your own. And you were just a kid, Deej. A kid. As lousy as it's been for me to feel like that, no kid should ever have to feel it. Especially not at home, with his father and brother. Then there was Allaire, and my getting her when you wanted her, and where were you again?"

"Odd man out," D.J. said.

"Right. Honest to God, I didn't have any idea how you felt about her and didn't mean you any harm, but it's no wonder you've hated my guts—"

"You're my brother. I haven't hated your guts."

"Damn close, though. And it's okay. I get it now. I know the feeling and it stinks and to have felt it as a kid and then to have had salt poured into the wound over Allaire... I'd have punched me out, too."

D.J. almost cracked a smile.

"But here's the thing," Dax continued. "There's nothing left to resent now. Your business is better than mine is. You have Allaire, and I'm not lying when I say I wish you both the best. So how about we really do try to put the past behind us and go from here?"

"Like brothers?"

"Yeah. Like brothers who may not have been friends growing up, but who can be friends now that we both know that life can kick the hell out of us so we don't have to kick the hell out of each other."

D.J. laughed. "Yeah, fighting like two hot-headed teenagers *was* pretty stupid."

Dax put his tongue far over on one side of his mouth and then said, "Yeah, I think you might have cracked a tooth."

But he said it jokingly and only made his brother chuckle again.

Then D.J. said, "So, we're okay?" as if he was having difficulty believing it.

"I'm okay. I guess you have to decide if *you're* okay since you're the one who's really gotten the short end of the stick up until now."

D.J. didn't answer in a hurry. He was clearly considering whether or not he *could* let go of so many years of hard feelings toward Dax, and Dax didn't push him.

But after a few minutes D.J. visibly relaxed, and he stoically nodded his head. "Let's put it all to rest," he seemed to decide on the spot. "What's past is past and we can go from here."

Dax held out his hand for his brother to shake and D.J. took it without hesitation.

"Everything all right here?"

Dax hadn't seen Grant return and didn't know if D.J. had, either.

"Everything's good," D.J. answered him, his eyes remaining on Dax, this time not suspiciously but with the first warmth Dax thought D.J. might ever have aimed at him.

"Everything's good," Dax repeated, his own gaze sticking with D.J. "Great, in fact."

"Seriously?" Grant said as if he needed convincing.

Their handshake ended and both Dax and D.J. looked at Grant.

"Seriously," D.J. said.

But as if the brothers had made a silent oath to keep what they'd just discussed between themselves, neither of them filled Grant in.

Grant, however, wasn't going to let it drop completely. "Does this mean that we can have our monthly poker games and dinners like the one before Thanksgiving without any tension?"

"That's what it means," Dax said.

"And no more weddings without everybody there?"

"That, too," D.J. answered their friend.

"We're gonna be all right, Grant. You can relax," Dax assured.

"Then that just leaves us to figure out what's come over you, Dax," Grant said.

Dax merely smiled a smile that gave nothing away before he stood to go.

It had been a long, long time since Dax had felt as buzzed as he did driving from the resort to his apartment after meeting with Grant and resolving things with D.J.

No, it wasn't the same adrenaline rush that came with winning a motorcycle race. But having Grant be receptive to his business proposition, seeing a doorway to the future open where before he'd seen only failure and, on top of that, paving a new road with his brother? It all left him closer to that high than he'd been in two years.

And again, even if he hadn't given Shandie the credit publicly, he didn't have any illusions about what she'd done for him and the fact that what had happened today was all thanks to her. In her own small, quiet way, she'd worked a miracle, and as soon as he could, he was going to tell her so.

It just wasn't going to be as soon as he would have liked.

Kayla's preschool winter program was tonight, and in the process of her mother painting the scenery for it in his garage on Saturday evening he'd been invited to go.

He'd accepted and because he was taking Shandie and Kayla to it he needed to get home, shower, shave and change clothes before he picked them up. So telling Shandie what she'd set into motion couldn't happen until then.

But at least then he'd be with her the way he'd been itching to be every minute since he'd walked out her door last night.

Grant had been right—something *had* happened to him.

Shandie Solomon had happened to him.

Being with her had somehow made him do a turnaround. A full one-eighty, so that he *was* different. He was more like his old self. Only better.

At least he *felt* better. He felt grounded. Centered. Solid. Stable.

He felt happy.

That almost came as a shock as he pulled into his driveway and headed for his upstairs apartment.

He felt *happy*.

His mail was on the floor in front of the mail slot when he let himself into his apartment. He picked it up and tossed it onto his kitchen table, not even glancing at it. He was too lost in the realization that he, Dax Traub, had just thought of himself as happy.

And not only because his business proposition for the resort looked as if it would pan out, he realized as he went straight to his bedroom and sloughed off his clothes.

Sure, that was terrific. But it struck him that even before Shandie had suggested his expansion, even before he'd decided to go to Grant with it, his black funk had begun to take a hike. Under Shandie's influence.

He turned on the water in the shower, gave it a minute to warm up, then stepped under the spray and closed the shower door behind him, wondering as he did when he'd started to feel better.

It hadn't happened the second he'd met Shandie, but he had to admit that he could track the turnaround back to that pivotal moment.

For days now, he hadn't been lying in bed after his alarm went off in the morning, dreading getting up. Instead, lately, the first thing he'd thought about was if or when or how he was going to get to see Shandie and Kayla again. And eagerness for that had lifted his spirits to such an extent that he'd been glad to get up and face the day.

And the nights? He hadn't been dropping his head onto his pillow, grateful to have put another day behind him so he could lose himself in sleep and escape. Since that first time he'd laid eyes on her he'd been going to sleep thinking about her. Picturing her in his mind, remembering things she'd said, her laugh, how bright her eyes were. He'd fallen asleep bathing himself in memories of the sound of her voice, reliving the touch of her hand, the feel of her lips, how soft her skin was under his fingertips.

Her positive outlook, her optimism, her energy were like some kind of tonic, he thought as he shampooed his hair. Better than any painkiller the doctors had given him after the accident. Better than any vitamin he'd ever taken. Better than anything that had come into his life since his first motorcycle.

But that wasn't all. And while he used a bar of soap to lather up, that realization settled over him.

Shandie wasn't merely some drug that boosted his mood. She wasn't like putting contacts in nearsighted eyes. The change in him that he attributed to her wasn't superficial —the way it had been with Lizbeth—and it wasn't only about how hot he was for Shandie.

It was honestly as if he'd been half a man, and she'd made him whole.

Oh yeah, tell Grant that! He'd laugh me out of town.

But it was the damn truth.

He finally felt like a complete person, and it was because of her. It was why he could let bygones be bygones with his brother. It was why he could put his failed marriage to Allaire behind him and genuinely not care that she was with D.J. now. It was why he could even recall the foolishness of his engagement to Lizbeth, see it for what it was, and put that behind him, too.

In a way, it occurred to him that everything that had come before Shandie had been nothing more than his going through the motions. With Allaire, when getting married was what they were expected to do, when it had seemed like the next step into adulthood, they'd gotten married. But they'd only been going through the motions of being adults.

With Lizbeth, he hadn't loved her. He hadn't wanted her or to marry her. He'd just gone through the motions that his friends, his brother were going through, in the hopes that putting the right surface on things would give him substance.

But now he *had* the substance.

Or at least he recognized what the substance was.

For him, it was Shandie. And how he felt about her. And the impact she had on him. And the man she inspired him to be. And what they had—and could have—together.

He rinsed off, shocked a second time by the direction his thoughts were taking. By the weight of what he was considering.

This really *wasn't* like things with Lizbeth, was it? he asked himself, faltering slightly.

But it didn't take much to convince him that it wasn't.

With Lizbeth he'd only barely risen above his dismal mood and then never for longer than when he was with her. That was nothing more than distraction. And the fact that he'd recognized that there wasn't anything else to it was what had prompted him to call off the engagement.

But with Shandie, there was no barely rising above his dismal mood when he was with her, only to sink into it again the minute he wasn't. She hadn't been anywhere around today when he'd opted to follow through on her idea for his business. He'd done that because being with her had recharged his own energy source, his own inner strength. That was what had allowed him to take the steps he'd taken today.

And had it not been successful? Would that have shot the hell out of what was between them? he asked himself as he stepped out of the shower and began to towel off.

It wouldn't have.

The same way he was eager to get to her and tell her the good news, had the news been bad she was who he would have wanted to share it with, too. Who he would have wanted to regroup with. To rehash with. To rethink the future with.

She was the good, but she was also where he would have wanted to turn had things gone sour. Because this wasn't about show. It wasn't about pretending things were all right in hopes that they would be. It wasn't about keeping up with his brother or his friends.

So no, this wasn't anything like what he'd gone through with Lizbeth. Even if his relationship with Shandie had developed in a hurry, the way that it had.

He was different as a result of Shandie because Shandie was different. His feelings for her were different. And even what he wanted was different because what he wanted didn't have a single thing to do with proving to his friends and his brother that he had his act together or that he was on top of things again. With Shandie, he *was* on top of things again. He *did* have his act together. And he couldn't have cared less whether anyone recognized it. He only cared that it was true. He only cared about Shandie.

And Kayla.

And having them in his life.

Both of them—because they were a package deal and that fact didn't even give him pause. Which was something else that told him what he was feeling was the genuine article and nothing like anything he'd felt before. In the past, a three-year-old coming along in the mix would have freaked him out. Yet he was as thrilled with the idea of having Kayla in his life as he was with thoughts of Shandie. They already felt like his family.

Except that they'd begun as someone else's family, he reminded himself. Someone Shandie had adored. Someone she might be remembering as bigger than life...

Could he compete with that? he asked himself as he pulled on a pair of clean jeans and a heavy mock-turtleneck sweater.

He may have had a moment's doubt when

he'd realized that what had developed between him and Shandie had happened as fast as his engagement to Lizbeth, but the thought of being compared to Shandie's late husband was more daunting.

Pete—that was his name. Said always in that sort of reverence used for a lost loved one.

Shandie *had* loved him. Deeply and without reservation.

Right to the end, Dax thought.

What if I can't live up to that?

He sank onto the edge of his bed, his socks left dangling, forgotten, from one hand as that possibility held him in its grip.

But he realized that if his father had been there with him he would have said that he was losing the race before he'd even hit the track and given it a try. And that was something he'd never let himself do on a motorcycle. It wasn't something he would let himself do now, when this was so much more important.

More important than a motorcycle race?

He *had* come a long way, he thought when that struck him.

But it was the truth. Shandie—and Kayla—were more important to him than any race he could remember. They were more important than anything in his life now. And he wasn't going to let that slip through his fingers. Not because of his past, or hers. And not even if he and Shandie *had* agreed that there would be no strings attached when this had begun.

Because now he *wanted* strings attached. Lots of them.

Chapter Ten

Shandie sat through Kayla's program Monday evening unsure what to think.

Not about the program in which her daughter was a snow fairy—Kayla did leaps and skips and preened hilariously, and was generally the star of the show.

No, what Shandie was at a loss for was an explanation of what was going on with Dax.

When he'd picked them up he'd announced that he had something to tell her. But Kayla had been so excited for the program that she'd chattered the entire way to the high school where the program was being held. She'd made it impossible for either Dax or Shandie to get a word in edgewise.

Then they'd arrived at the school and Dax had had to find them seats in the auditorium while Shandie went backstage with Kayla and the set decorations, and helped out behind the scenes. Shandie had barely found her place beside him before the program began, so again—although he'd repeated that he wanted to talk to her—he hadn't had the chance.

And she was expecting the worst.

He was acting a little strange. He was less laid back than usual. Slightly more wired. More antsy. And several times she'd caught him watching her so intently she knew he wasn't paying attention to what was going on around him. It all caused her to wonder if he was about to break things off with her.

Oh, sure, he was still being nice enough. He'd made a few jokes. He was patient with Kayla and very kind to her even in the midst of Kayla's hyper-excitement. But something was up and Shandie knew it. And given his history with women, it just seemed likely that this was about to be it for them.

One fantastic roll in the hay and the guy was out the door for good, she thought. In fact, as the program went on, he was so distracted that she wondered if he'd intended to end things between them the minute he'd gotten to her house so he wouldn't have to go through with this evening, and just hadn't managed it.

But if what he had in mind was breaking up with her, why had he just reached over and taken her hand to hold?

Maybe that was just part of how he did it. Maybe the hand-holding was meant to be comforting or supportive before he lowered the boom.

It didn't seem like consolation hand-holding, though. It seemed very intimate. Especially since he had them situated so snugly. His upper arm was resting against the front of hers, tucking her shoulder behind his. His elbow rode the inner curve of hers. Their forearms were inside to inside. It all felt close and cozy and couple-ish. But still, she had a sense of impending doom.

It's okay, Shandie told herself. *If he's going to end it, fine. I just have to be prepared. I knew it was going to happen sooner or later. Better sooner than later. It's the price to pay for getting involved with someone I know is a high risk when it comes to relationships.*

*No strings attached, remember? That was
the deal...*

She took a slow, deep breath and exhaled
it just as slowly.

It was for the best not to go any further, she
insisted to herself. The lovemaking had been
too good. Any more of it and she knew she
would get in deeper than she should. Deep
enough to be hurt. Seriously hurt. By a man
she'd known all along wasn't someone with
staying power. Better to have only one night
before he called it quits than to end up engaged to him, announcing that engagement,
and *then* have him break up with her—like
he had with Lizbeth Stanton.

The program concluded just then; all the
preschool classes filed onto the stage and
the need to clap gave Shandie the excuse
to snatch her hand from Dax's as they both
joined in the applause.

*Definitely better to get this over with be-
fore it's too late,* she thought.

But she was no longer looking forward
to the post-show ice cream that was being
served in the cafeteria. She was too worried
that that would be when she'd finally hear
what Dax had to say.

And regardless of what she told herself,

imagining that what had developed between them was about to end already made her feel awful....

"I wan' yur ice cream," Kayla said.

She, Dax and Shandie were in the school cafeteria, sitting at the end of a long table— Dax on one side, Shandie on the other and the still-hyper Kayla kneeling on the table itself, rocking back and forth with the excess of energy that hadn't yet been spent.

The three-year-old was dressed in pink corduroy overalls and a white blouse with ruffles around the Peter Pan collar. She also still had on the filmy fairy wings that had been her costume for the program because she refused to take them off. They were held on by straps around her shoulders, like a backpack, and since most of the other kids continued to wear face paint or some remnant of their own homemade costume, Shandie wasn't fighting to get Kayla to take off her wings.

Besides, Shandie didn't have much fight in her. Not with what was lingering on her mind—the same thoughts that had occupied her during the program. They'd also robbed her of her appetite, so she hadn't taken any ice cream and she noted that Dax had barely touched his. Which seemed as if he might also have something weighty on *his* mind.

For her part, Kayla seemed only to notice the ice cream that wasn't being eaten.

"That's Dax's," Shandie said to her daughter as the child inched toward the plastic cup that held about half of his scoop of vanilla.

"But he's not eatin' it and iss meltin'."

"I'm finished. She can have it," Dax said with an indulgent chuckle before Shandie could address Kayla's comment. Then, to Kayla, he added, "If it's okay with your mom."

"Iss okay," Kayla decreed, scooting on her knees to get nearer to her goal.

"It's okay, but only if you get off the table the way I've told you twice already," Shandie said.

Kayla complied promptly this time, but for some reason slid off into Dax's lap rather than onto the bench beside him.

"Kayla!" Shandie exclaimed when a surprised Dax barely caught her. "You're out of control tonight and that's enough!"

Dax laughed. "She's all right," he assured her, situating the little girl so she could use his chest as her backrest, her fairy wings splayed out behind her.

"I'm a'right," the three-year-old repeated.

Being in Dax's lap did seem to finally calm her down because she concentrated on finishing his ice cream and was suddenly—and blissfully—quiet.

And because Shandie was on pins and needles in anticipation of Dax's saying it was time to count him out of this threesome, she said, "Maybe if little ones can be seen and not heard for a few minutes you can tell me what you wanted to tell me when you first picked us up tonight."

Dax craned his head forward to peer down at Kayla. "I'm only averaging about two words in that direction before she gets started again," he joked. "I'm not sure the odds are in my favor."

"It's okay if you want to wait," Shandie said, thinking that maybe hearing what he had to say in private *would* be preferable because she was less and less sure she was going to be able to control her emotions.

Dax looked down at Kayla again. The child honestly did seem to have run out of steam and that must have convinced him because he raised his espresso-colored eyes to Shandie and said, "I did it."

"You did what?" she asked.

"Both of 'em, actually," he added cryptically.

Shandie raised her eyebrows in query and he explained.

"I thought about everything you said about expanding my business and I went to see Grant today. I laid it all out for him—snowmobiles, ATVs, the possibility of my guiding guests into the backcountry, the whole deal."

"And?" Shandie said.

"I'm in," he announced with a proud grin that stretched his supple mouth nearly ear to ear. "Grant jumped at the idea, added a few touches of his own, and we're gonna to do business."

"Congratulations!" Shandie said, pleased for him but still wary.

"Then, at the end of my talking to Grant, D.J. walked in and I called a truce with him, too."

More good news. Why did she continue to feel as if another shoe was going to drop?

But what she said was, "How did that go?"

"Pretty well, everything considered. D.J. was kind of leery at first, but I convinced him it was time for us both to turn over a new leaf. I told him that I understand how he felt—like the odd man out—and that now that I've had some time in that spot myself, I can relate, that I didn't like it. What I said seemed to strike a nerve with him, as if my finally getting what he'd felt for so long and recognizing that there was a reason for his resentment went a long way in making him feel better. And he accepted the truce."

"I'm so glad for you," Shandie said without reservation on that score.

"And it's all thanks to you," he said then. "I have to apologize for not letting Grant—or D.J., either—in on that, though. Eventually, I promise, I'll make sure you get the credit, but it didn't seem smart to tell Grant, in particular, that the whole business idea came from the woman I'm seeing. I was afraid if he knew he might think I wasn't fully committed or something—the way things were when I was with Lizbeth and wasn't making levelheaded decisions and didn't follow through with things."

"I don't need any credit," Shandie said, meaning it. "I just planted the seeds, you took it from there."

"The business expansion and making the connection with the resort was still your idea, and I won't forget that."

That sounded like something someone might say as a lead-up to the announcement that they were moving on.

Was she just being paranoid?

The man *did* have a history...

"You had a busy day," she observed, watching him, looking for signs that there was more to come.

"To tell you the truth, it was another slow day—that's when I decided to go to Grant. But, yeah, once I put those wheels into motion I accomplished a lot. I also did a lot of thinking to go with it," he finished in what was obviously a segue.

"So there's more," she said tentatively.

"As a matter of fact, the business stuff, the truce with D.J., were just where things started. From there—"

Shandie lunged across the cafeteria table just in time to catch the ice cream dish.

At some point, while Shandie and Dax were talking, Kayla had fallen asleep with the plastic cup in one hand and the spoon in the other. Had Shandie not acted with split-second reflexes, soupy ice cream would have ended up all over Dax.

Dax's eyes shot to Kayla again, too, surprised to find she'd nodded off.

"We should get her home," he said when Shandie had taken the plastic cup out of harm's way and removed the spoon from Kayla's hand, too. "We can talk about the rest after we get this kiddo to bed."

The rest...

The knot in Shandie's stomach tightened.

She moved as if through a fog then. With Dax still holding Kayla, Shandie took off the fairy wings, slipped her sleeping child's arms into her coat, pulled up the hood and zipped her in. She deposited the ice cream dishes in the trash and put on her own jacket over the slacks and sweater set she was wearing.

Once that was accomplished, she held Kayla while Dax shrugged on his own coat and then she let him take Kayla back to carry out to his truck.

And through it all, through the short drive to her house, she just kept thinking, *Don't cry, whatever you do, don't cry...*

It was a mantra she continued even after they'd arrived at her place, and the whole time she was undressing Kayla and getting her to bed.

Don't cry and embarrass yourself. Don't let him see that he's gotten to you so soon. Don't cry, whatever you do, don't cry...

Dax was waiting for her in the living room when she went downstairs with her hands clenched into tense fists in her pockets, as if that would help her keep some control. She didn't offer him tea or coffee or a nightcap, she didn't join him on the sofa where he sat at an angle, one arm stretched across the top of the cushions in back. She just stopped as she reached the rear of the easy chair and said, "So tell me the rest," hating that her voice came out so small.

"The rest is about you and me," he said.

"I thought it might be."

He must have found her dire tone puzzling because his expression reflected that. But he didn't say anything about it. He just patted the seat next to him and said, "Come and sit down."

"I'm okay here."

More confusion.

"Tell me the rest," Shandie said quietly, thinking that she couldn't bear the wait any longer.

Still clearly confused, he complied in spite of it.

"I came out of the resort today feeling like I was on top of the world. And even though I hadn't let Grant or D.J. know how much of what had just happened was due to you, *I* knew it. All I could think about was rushing to you to share it and… Well, that's when it hit me—I want to share everything with you. From here on in. It hit me that for the first time in my life I feel like I'm—"

He shook his head and rolled his eyes. "This sounds so sappy," he said.

But then he continued, anyway. "For the first time in my life I feel like I've found a part of me that's been missing. Something that fills a gap I didn't even know was there, and makes me…I'm not even sure how to put it into words…makes me centered, grounded. And coming from that, I can see beyond myself so I can deal with what needs to be dealt with, with a clearer perspective. Without giving it more weight than it deserves because no matter what it is, the only thing that *really* matters is this core that's here now. This core that's been formed by you and me coming together. It's you, Shandie, who fills the gap, who's more important—so important—that as long as there's you, everything else can work out or not work out, can be there or not be there, and I know I can still go on perfectly fine. As long as I have you."

He shook his head again, this time in astonishment. "And what I realized when it hit me is that I need to hang on to that. I need to hang on to you. Tight."

So he wasn't breaking up with her. In fact, he was saying wonderful things.

But rather than feeling relieved and excited by his words, Shandie was wondering if, not so long ago, he'd claimed similar sentiments for Lizbeth Stanton. If this was the same kind of heat-of-the-moment thing that had inspired his impetuous proposal to the other woman...

"What is it about tonight that has everybody so wound up?" she said, trying to make a joke. "First Kayla and now you."

"I am wound up," Dax confessed. "This has been a great day and the start of a great future. And I want you in on it."

"I'm thrilled that it was a great day for you—you deserve it. I think—and hope—it *is* the start of a great future for you, too. But other than that, maybe you should slow down, take a breath, just enjoy this without barreling into anything else."

"I want to barrel into something else," he insisted. "I know this is impulsive, but it's a good impulse. I can feel it in my bones."

Shandie didn't say anything. She doubted it would have much more effect on him than anything she'd said to Kayla tonight to try to get her daughter to calm down.

"Come on," he urged, patting the couch cushion again. "Sit down and talk to me."

She gave him that much. She went to the sofa and sat down. But she sat as far from him as she could manage because she had no doubt that if there was any contact it would cloud her thinking.

"I know this is all quick," he said then, correctly translating the distance she was keeping as a sign of her own reservation. "It struck me like a bolt of lightning, too. But once it did, I just knew it was the way things should be. That we should be together. A family."

"Slow down, Dax," Shandie repeated softly.

"I don't want to slow down. I don't see any reason to slow down. I've thought it all through, Shandie. You told me yourself that I had to figure out what makes me happy now that what made me happy before is gone— well, I figured that out today—"

"What made you happy today was having Grant like the business proposition you went to him with, and making up with your brother."

"No. What I figured out today was that I was feeling happy before any of that happened. That I've been feeling happier and happier the longer things have gone on with you. That *you* have been making me happy. You and Kayla and being with you both. What I figured out today was that if Grant *hadn't* liked the idea, if he'd blown me out of the water, *you* are still who I would have wanted to turn to. That you are who I want to be with whether things are good or bad or just plugging along. *That's* when I knew that this—" he waved a long index finger back and forth between them "—that whatever this is that's happened with us is the only damn thing that makes any difference to anything."

It was Shandie shaking her head now. "That's nice but—"

"You don't feel the same way."

"I haven't thought about it like that," she admitted. "This is so new—what's happening with us—and..." And she'd only been thinking that if he had something he wanted to talk about, it must be that he didn't want to see her anymore.

"To tell you the truth," she said, deciding on the spot to do just that, "I thought you were going to say we should cool it."

"Cool it? Like stop seeing each other?"

Shandie nodded.

"Why would I have wanted to say that?"

She shrugged.

"Because of Lizbeth," he guessed. "You thought this was like that—some fling that I'd already lost interest in."

"The whole thing with Lizbeth Stanton was a whirlwind romance that you were gung ho about and then called off. And there has been that talk around the Clip 'n Curl about my being *the next Lizbeth*—"

"I told you I was only 'gung ho' about things with Lizbeth on the surface. That it was all a stupid attempt to fix what was wrong by just making it *seem* as if it was fixed."

"And this isn't the same?" Shandie asked.

"No, this isn't the same!" he answered with absolute conviction.

But regardless of how convinced he might be, Shandie wasn't. And suddenly all the things she'd been imagining during the program and worrying about and dreading and trying to prepare herself for had a new and different significance.

Because she *wasn't* sure if she might not just be "the next Lizbeth Stanton." And it had taken only a slight change in Dax's mood and the simple statement that he had something to tell her for her to fall into thinking he was going to end things with her. For her to be completely on edge. On the verge of tears, even. To give her a sense of impending doom. To suck the fun out of an evening that she should have enjoyed.

Wasn't that what she would be facing if she went on being involved with Dax in whatever way he saw them involved in the future? she asked herself. Wouldn't the slightest change in him leave her thinking all the same things she'd thought tonight? Wouldn't that always be hanging over her head? Only wouldn't feeling what she'd felt tonight get even harder as more time passed? After they'd made love again and again? When she was counting on his being around? Wouldn't everything she'd felt tonight be a hundred times harder?

Then into her mind's eye came the image of Kayla plopping comfortably down into Dax's lap the way she had earlier in the evening. She could see her daughter once more snuggled against him, feeling confident in him, feeling so safe and secure that she'd fallen asleep in his arms. And she could only think about how much worse it would be for them both for him to change his mind later and leave them behind.

Sooner or later—that's what she'd thought just a little while ago—Dax's ending this relationship was inevitable, and that if that was the case, it was better sooner than later.

But how long was she going to wait for later to come? Fearing every slight variation in Dax's attitude and knowing that when the ax fell, she wasn't the only one who would feel the blow?

That wasn't something to embrace. It wasn't even something to accept. And even if she were willing to consider accepting it for herself, she didn't have only herself to think about. She had Kayla.

"I don't know what you're thinking, Dax," she began. "But it won't work."

His puzzlement returned to carve deep grooves into his forehead. "If you don't know what I'm thinking how can you know it won't work?"

"I'm just saying that this—" she mimicked him waving a finger back and forth between them "—won't work."

"Why not? It seems like it's been working great."

"Until tonight," she said more to herself than to him.

"What was wrong with tonight?" he asked, baffled.

"I've been…I've been so sure that this was it, that this was where my being 'the next Lizbeth' would happen, that I've felt *awful.*" She infused the word with the misery she'd been suffering.

"But that isn't what happened."

"No, not tonight. But when? Next week? Next month? Next year? Or the next? I can't go through worrying and wondering and being afraid of when it *will* happen."

"Maybe it *won't* happen—did that occur to you?"

It hadn't and she admitted it. "But the odds aren't in my favor," she said. "Your track record, your reputation—"

"All come from the past. From my history with other people. From making choices that were made too young or for the wrong reasons," he qualified.

"But there's a pattern there," Shandie insisted.

"A pattern that makes me a bad risk."

"A pattern that says the way Allaire ended up, the way Lizbeth Stanton did, are likely the way I'd end up, too. And I have Kayla to think about because she'd go through her own share of misery."

"Nobody knows better than I do that I've already had one failed marriage and that I acted like an ass in rushing into that engagement with Lizbeth for all the wrong reasons, Shandie. Or that those two rash acts don't make me highly recommendable. But this—" he did the finger waving again "—is nothing like either of those other two times. I'm not barely more than a teenager, the way I was with Allaire. And as for Lizbeth—yeah, there's the speed issue in that this is as whirlwind as it was with her. But it's the *feelings* that are different. There's no show here. I didn't even tell Grant or D.J. about you. Nothing about this is to prove anything to anyone. This is about you and me. And Kayla, who I swear to you, I would never, ever do anything to hurt."

"Oh, Dax…" Shandie sighed.

"Don't 'Oh, Dax' me like that. I know what I'm talking about. I *feel* different about you than I did about Lizbeth. I feel more different about you than I have about anyone in my life. Yes, it's happened fast, but it's still real—the real thing you said I haven't ever actually felt. Well, now I have. Now I'm feeling it. And you're right because it isn't anything like what I felt before. That's how I know this can work out. That this can go the distance."

"You've just had your first big victory in a long time," she reasoned. "Don't you think that what you're feeling could be part of that?"

"I think it's separate from that. That that's just the frosting on the cake—and you're the cake."

He was boring into her with those dark eyes, his unbelievably gorgeous face tight with the tension she'd created, and she could see that she was taking the joy out of this day for him. She regretted that. But there was more at stake. For her. For Kayla. And Shandie couldn't let herself lose sight of that.

"I can't just jump into anything," she said.

"Didn't you just jump into selling your house in Denver, uprooting yourself and Kayla to move here, and investing in your cousin's business?"

"I didn't just jump into any of that, no. I made changes, yes, but—"

"You don't consider it taking a chance to invest money in a business that's been seeing a recent decline?"

"It isn't the same, Dax."

"You took that chance, Shandie. So take a chance on me."

In spite of what he was saying, Shandie didn't see moving to Thunder Canyon, buying into the struggling Clip 'n Curl, as comparable to what he was asking of her. Failure on either count couldn't wound her. It couldn't scar her daughter. The consequences were so much more easily fixed if those things didn't work out. But a relationship with Dax? An attempt at a future with him? If *that* didn't work out it could do genuine damage.

Shandie shook her head again. "No," she said quietly, feeling every bit as bad at that moment as she'd expected to feel tonight when she'd been so sure Dax would be breaking up with her.

But if this is how bad it feels now, how much worse would it feel if I was in even deeper?

"You married a man you knew might not have a long life ahead of him, but you won't give me a chance because of things that are totally in the past?" he said incredulously.

He had a point, of course. But still—or maybe because of that—it sent a wave of anger through her.

"When I married Pete, I was the only one I was putting out there on the limb. That isn't how it is now," she said stiffly.

"So I'm crazy about your daughter and *you're* making her the downfall of this?" he asked as if he couldn't fathom that.

But Shandie wasn't going to argue that. "I just can't, Dax. Your track record is too scary."

"Look at me," he ordered. "I'm *not* scary."

She did look at him, and it nearly broke her heart to see that face that sent tingles all through her and still know she had to stand her ground.

"Your history is," she said.

"And history repeats itself," he mocked sarcastically.

"I can't risk finding out," she nearly whispered, as her anger receded behind a rise of panic.

He took a turn shaking his head once more, staring at her as if he were at a loss.

"You don't mean that," he said then, giving it one more try.

"I do. I have to," she told him, even though she didn't want to. Even though she wished she could do anything else.

But tonight and feeling the way she had

wasn't something she wanted to do again. It wasn't something she wanted forever looming in the background. And even if she had any illusions that she might be able to handle it, she couldn't and wouldn't put her daughter in a position that could potentially cause the little girl pain.

"So I come to you with great news and hope for the future and you kick me out?" Dax challenged.

"I just can't be a part of it from here on in," Shandie said.

"You *won't* be," he accused.

He gave her another moment under the penetrating scrutiny of those piercing eyes, but Shandie didn't waver.

Then he stood, grabbed his coat from the arm of the easy chair with a fierce swipe and stalked out of her house.

In the silence that he left behind, Shandie just sat there on the couch.

She'd felt bad when she'd said no to him. She hadn't expected the feelings to grow bigger and stronger still once he was gone.

But there they were, welling up in her, nearly strangling her, filling her eyes with hot, stinging tears.

And that was when she wondered if she'd been fooling herself.

If she was already in this further than she'd thought.

Chapter Eleven

"Kayla Jane Solomon, don't do this to me..."

Shandie muttered the plea to herself Friday evening when she went to the Clip 'n Curl's break room to get her daughter in order to go home for the day. What she found was the little girl's DVD playing but no one watching it.

"Where are you, Kayla?" Shandie called in a voice loud enough to be heard throughout the deserted salon.

It would have been too easy had Kayla come running or popped out of a hiding place or called back from the restroom. But no, only silence answered Shandie and she knew why. It was the same thing that had been causing her problems for the past four days—Kayla had slipped through the utility room to go to Dax again.

"Why couldn't you just cut me a little slack this once, Kayla?" Shandie lamented, leaning wearily against the break room's doorjamb and closing her eyes.

She was so tired. She hadn't slept more than two or three hours a night since everything with Dax had gone up in smoke. She hadn't eaten much, either, and with all the stress and strain and late-night crying on top of it, she was a wreck. She was certainly not in any shape to see Dax.

But she didn't have a doubt that the motorcycle shop was where her daughter was. Not only had it become a pattern this week, but with the other salon doors locked while Shandie cleaned up after closing, it was the only place Kayla *could* be.

Shandie hadn't been sure how to handle Kayla after the breakup. It had seemed as if the split would be a bigger deal if she made a special point of sitting the three-year-old down first thing Tuesday morning and announcing that Dax would no longer be coming around. Besides, all through Monday night Shandie had hoped Kayla might not even notice his absence, leaving nothing to explain.

But of course Kayla had noticed. She might have even sensed that something had gone wrong because, over breakfast Tuesday, the three-year-old had started asking when they were going to see Dax again.

Shandie had been honest with her daughter, but she'd played it down. She'd told Kayla that they probably *wouldn't* be seeing Dax again. She'd reminded her daughter that they'd talked about how Dax might not be a forever-friend, and how now it seemed as if that was going to be the case. That Dax would be going on about his business and they would be going on about theirs, and there wasn't any reason for them all to get together anymore.

Kayla had not accepted any of that as the last word. She'd demanded to know why. She'd refuted Shandie's every stock answer and insisted that she liked Dax and wanted him to be their forever-friend. Then, in direct rebellion of her mother, every chance she'd found this week, the three-year-old had snuck through the utility room to the motorcycle shop.

Asking her nicely not to do that, offering her bribes if she didn't, threatening punishment if she did and ultimately taking away cookies and television for continuing to do it had all failed to stop the stubborn child from her determined pursuit of maintaining contact with Dax.

Shandie had requested that the contractor in charge of the Clip 'n Curl's remodel change the handle on the door that connected the garage to the salon so it could be locked, but that had yet to be done. And now Kayla had again disappeared from the salon. Only, to make it even worse, there were no fellow stylists to take pity on Shandie and retrieve her daughter for her—as there had been on every other occasion.

Tonight, Shandie was going to have to do it herself.

And come face-to-face with Dax for the first time since Monday night.

She really, really didn't want to do that.

"Kayla Jane Solomon, where are you!" she shouted as loudly as she was capable, hoping that her voice might carry all the way to the motorcycle shop and that the three-year-old would return on her own.

Then Shandie opened her eyes and waited, listening for any indication that the little girl was answering the call.

But there wasn't a single sound. And Shandie knew she was going to have to go over there.

The thought of it made her want to crawl into a shell. She didn't know how it had happened so quickly, but she felt more for Dax than she'd realized until he'd walked out of her house Monday night. Before that she'd honestly believed her feelings for him were under control. That she liked him—a lot—but not so much that it was anywhere near what she'd felt for Pete.

Then Dax had left, and in the past four days the agony Shandie had been going through was close enough to what she'd gone through when Pete had died for her to take a second look at her feelings for Dax. And to discover that she cared much, much more than she'd thought.

But that didn't change her mind about being with him. He was still the guy with the rotten track record with women. The guy who got into relationships unwisely or on whims or because of peer pressure, and then got out of them when the bloom was off the rose.

And she still had Kayla to protect from being hurt.

So with her mind unchanged about chancing a future with him, Shandie decided she had to stick to her guns.

This, too, will pass—that's what she kept telling herself at her darkest moments this week. Like her grief over Pete, as miserable as she was without Dax, it would eventually go away. And *then* maybe she would be able to stand to see him. At a distance.

But not now. Please, not now...

Only now her daughter was at Dax's shop with him, and she was going to have to see him.

"Tomorrow I'm putting a lock on that door myself!" she vowed, angry at Kayla, angry at the contractor, angry at herself for getting involved with Dax in the first place.

Just go and get it over with, she told herself, pushing off the doorjamb and heading for the utility room.

Every step that took her closer to the motorcycle shop made her heart race faster.

Would he be rude and obnoxious? she wondered. Would he be flip and smart-alecky? A wise guy? Would he be angry? Hostile? Or did he even care anymore? With his history, maybe he had never genuinely cared— regardless of what he'd said—and so he could get over these kinds of things without any problem...

None of the possibilities made the walk through the utility room easier on Shandie, but with no other option, once she reached the connecting door—which was wide open—she knocked on it and said, "Kayla, are you here?"

"She's here," came the answer in the familiar deep voice that just made Shandie ache inside.

She couldn't tell from those two simple words, though, what she was going to find when she got through the garage to the showroom, so she still went with a knot in the pit of her stomach.

Dax and Kayla were sitting at the table beside the sales counter where Dax took customers to do paperwork when he made a sale. Shandie aimed her gaze directly at her daughter, only peripherally aware that Dax was leaning back, feet propped on the table itself, ankles crossed, balancing on the rear two legs of his chair.

Kayla was perched on the second chair, her legs underneath her.

"I'm talkin' ta Dax," the three-year-old announced defensively when her mother neared.

"You're supposed to be waiting for me in the break room," Shandie countered tightly.

"I wanna'd ta talk ta Dax."

Dax let his chair drop to all four legs then, dragged his feet off the table and stood.

"Hi," he said to Shandie as if he thought she might intend not to address him at all.

She didn't know what she'd intended to do so he could have been right. But now she had to. She also had to look straight at him.

"Hi," she echoed quietly as she was slammed with the full-on sight of him and what it did to her.

He was dressed in a pair of disreputably age-worn jeans that would have looked like rags on anyone else but were sexy as all get-out on him. He was also wearing a plain white T-shirt under a denim jacket, which only added to his appeal.

And he *was* appealing. With his dark brown hair rebelliously disheveled and the shadow of a beard lending a scruffiness to his starkly handsome face, and those intense eyes boring into her, it was all enough to make Shandie want badly to close the distance between them, throw herself into his arms and say, *Forget everything, I just want you...*

But of course she wouldn't let herself do that. Instead, very stiltedly, she said, "I'm sorry she keeps coming over here and bothering you."

"She isn't bothering me. I'm always glad to see her."

Okay, so he was just going to be nice. Damn him. At least if he'd been a jerk it would have given her an excuse to grab her daughter and get out of there. Nice was so much more difficult than rude or obnoxious or wiseass. Nice she liked...

"I've picked up the phone a hundred times since Monday to call you," he said then.

Shandie didn't need to know that. She didn't want to know that. It only made it harder. And she didn't have a clue what to say in response to that information.

"I heard through the grapevine that you were busy signing contracts with the resort and ordering snowmobiles and ATVs," she said, repeating the talk that had circulated through the Clip 'n Curl in the past four days.

"I was. But it didn't help," he confided.

She also didn't need or want to know he might have been hurting the way she was.

"It's good, though, that things are getting going for you," she said too brightly.

"Yeah," he allowed. Then he seemed to try a different tack. "I understand Kayla Jane here is going to a sleepover tonight."

"At Bethany's," Kayla offered from the sidelines.

It didn't alter Dax's focus on Shandie. "Maybe we could have dinner. Talk…"

He would never know how much she wanted to say yes to that. So much that she couldn't say no, she had to merely shake her head to turn him down.

But he didn't give up. "You're the idea person and I could use a couple of good ones," he said, slowly closing the gap between them until he was standing directly in front of her.

"I'm sure you have ideas of your own," Shandie said as the blood seemed to pound in her ears.

"None that seem like they'll work," he claimed.

He carefully—and just barely—pressed his flattened palms to her arms, sliding down to her wrists where he took her hands in his.

"See," he said for her ears only, "there's this person I'm crazy about and I've been racking my brain for a way to convince her that—"

The touch of his hands, the faint smell of

his cologne, just having him so close made Shandie panic. If he kept this up she knew she'd never be able to hold on to her resolves, and she needed to. She *needed* to…

She shook her head vehemently again, stepped away from him and shot her gaze to her child once more. "Come on, Kayla. We need to get home," she said firmly.

"Le's eat dinner wis Dax first," Kayla suggested.

"No, we have dinner waiting at home and then you have to get to Bethany's."

"But I wanna be wis Dax," Kayla whined.

So do I…

But neither one of them could be, Shandie reminded herself. For their own good, neither one of them could be.

"Not tonight," she told her daughter.

"When? Tomorrow?"

"No."

"The nex' tomorrow?"

"Just come on, Kayla. Right now," Shandie ordered.

"I wanna stay here wis Dax. Pul-eee-ze…"

Shandie went to her daughter, picked up the child and held her slung on her hip.

"I wanna stay wis Dax," Kayla complained

with a quivering bottom lip. "Why can' we see him no more? I wanna. I yike Dax!"

"It's okay, Kayla," he soothed. "I'll see you again."

"I wanna see you now!" Kayla wailed pitifully as Shandie headed for the garage and made a beeline through it to the connecting door.

But before she could disappear into the utility room Dax's voice stopped her, coming from the entrance to the showroom.

"How is it better to play it safe if it makes us all this sad, Shandie?"

Shandie didn't answer him.

She didn't look back.

She just took her sobbing child away.

By seven o'clock Friday night Shandie had calmed her daughter, fed Kayla dinner, delivered her to the sleepover at Bethany's house and was back home alone for the evening.

She'd already decided that the best way to get through tonight would be to keep herself busy. Without Kayla underfoot, cleaning the child's room seemed like a productive way to spend the time.

She had the television blaring from her own bedroom so she could hear it in hopes that that would keep her mind occupied with something other than thoughts of Dax as she plunged into the three-year-old's room.

First up was to strip the bed and change the sheets. Off came the pink princess-themed quilt and the plain blanket under it. Then Shandie grabbed Kayla's pillow.

Doing that sent something flat to fall between the mattress and the headboard. Assuming it was a storybook or a coloring book that had provided some post–lights-out entertainment and then found its way under the pillow, Shandie retrieved it.

But it wasn't a book of any kind. It was something in a frame.

With the back side facing her when she took it from behind the mattress, Shandie didn't recognize the frame as one of hers and wondered what this was and where her daughter might have gotten it.

Then she flipped it over.

Stunned by what she saw, she sank down onto Kayla's bed.

It was a picture of Dax.

He was dressed in racing gear, a helmet tucked under one arm, proudly holding the trophy from winning a motorcycle race in the other.

Although Shandie didn't recognize that particular photograph, she knew where it had come from. The largest solid wall in the motorcycle shop was covered floor-to-|ceiling with similar pictures interspersed with memorabilia, magazine covers and newspaper headlines. All from Dax's motorcycle racing days.

Dax had called it his wall of credibility and said it was to make customers aware of the fact that he knew what he was talking about when it came to bikes.

Kayla must have snatched this picture off that wall.

Shandie had a vague memory of her daughter behaving a bit strangely about her backpack the day before—the three-year-old had insisted that she carry it herself, running upstairs with it the minute they'd arrived home last night rather than leaving it in the middle of the floor for Shandie to put away. Shandie hadn't thought much about it, but that must have been when Kayla had taken the picture—after preschool on one of Thursday's sneaky forays to the motorcycle shop. Then the little girl must have hidden it in her backpack in order to get it home. To hide under her pillow.

Shandie wasn't happy to find that her daughter had lifted someone else's property, but more than that, she felt awful that Kayla had wanted a picture of Dax—something to remind her of him—so badly she'd been willing to steal it. And that, coupled with Kayla's desire to see him, her distraught tantrum over being taken away from him tonight, all gave Shandie pause.

Clearly Kayla, too, already cared more for Dax than Shandie had thought.

She'd been so mired in her own pain and misery, Shandie guessed she hadn't realized how much her daughter was suffering and missing Dax, too. But thinking back on the past four days, on Kayla's unusual moodiness, on how easy it had been to set off crying jags and tantrums, Shandie was suddenly struck by the truth of it—Kayla was going through her own breakup angst.

"This is just what I was trying to avoid," Shandie said as if her daughter were there to hear her.

Playing it safe apparently didn't have much to recommend it. In order not to run the risk of being hurt later, she'd caused Kayla pain now.

With that spinning around in her brain,

Shandie stared down at the picture of Dax. He was obviously several years younger, but age and a few added lines had only made him better looking, and she couldn't resist caressing his image with her fingertips.

When had she become this person who played it safe? she wondered. Certainly that hadn't been the case with Pete. If she'd been playing it safe with him, she would have run the other way as soon as he'd been honest about his health problems and the very real possibility that his cancer could return a third—and more serious—time.

Certainly there had been people then— more than a few—who had advised her against marrying Pete. Who had thought she was out of her mind to try to have a future with a man who might not have long to live. And when the worst had happened with Pete, there had been those same people and more— one even at his funeral—who had said, "I told you so."

But then, even that day, Shandie hadn't regretted that she'd taken the chance on Pete. They might not have had long together, but what they'd had had been worth it. Having Kayla had been worth it.

"If I had played it safe then," Shandie said

to Dax's photograph, "I would have spared myself a lot of pain, but I also would have lost out on what I *did* have with him."

But she'd followed her heart when it came to Pete, and she'd never been sorry for that. Not even through the worst of the grief had she regretted that she'd married him.

Yet here she was now, playing it safe, trying to avoid something that might happen in order to spare herself and Kayla pain, and causing them pain in the process.

How was that better? she thought, recalling Dax's parting shot.

She wasn't sure she could answer it, but she couldn't help wondering if Lizbeth Stanton could.

And being the "next Lizbeth Stanton" was a major part of what she'd been trying to avoid.

So, would the other woman agree with the playing-it-safe course and say that Shandie and Kayla were better dealing with this now than later, the way Lizbeth Stanton had been forced to when Dax had broken their engagement?

Shandie honestly didn't know.

But she *did* know that regardless of what Lizbeth Stanton had felt when the relationship ended, the other woman was no worse for wear now. Shandie had met her at the pre-Thanksgiving dinner, she'd seen the other woman with her new fiancé, and Lizbeth Stanton appeared to be extremely happy now.

So did Allaire, Dax's ex-wife, for that matter.

Both women had weathered the breakup with Dax and come through it just fine.

And what if it's true that what he feels for me is different than what he felt for either of them? What if what he feels for me is the real thing and I didn't even give him the benefit of the doubt? The chance?

Then she *was* suffering and causing Kayla to suffer for no reason. And that was a hard pill to swallow.

"I'm sorry if that's what I've done, Kayla," she said, fighting another stab at the thought that any action she'd taken might have inadvertently hurt her daughter, who hadn't had the slightest say in what was going on.

And Shandie knew what Kayla would have said if she'd been consulted about what had gone on with Dax. Kayla would have said the same thing she'd said at the motorcycle shop tonight—that she wanted to be with Dax *now*.

Kayla was three. Living in the moment was what she did. And even though it was Shandie's job to look beyond the moment, maybe this time that wasn't what she should be doing. Maybe this time living in the moment was the way to go. The same way it had been with Pete.

After all, what she'd had with Dax until she'd turned her back on it hadn't been only good for Dax. Or for Kayla. It had been good for Shandie, too, she admitted to herself. She'd been genuinely happy with him. She'd been enjoying—more than enjoying—every minute with him. She certainly hadn't felt as if what was going on between them was superficial or just for show. It had felt like the real thing to her. And if there hadn't been substance to it, how had she come as far with him as she had in such a short while?

But she'd nixed the possibility of that continuing because of what had happened between him and other women. Because of what other people were saying about him, about his relationship with her.

Didn't that make her the one who was guilty of superficiality? Of letting outside forces rule? She hadn't let that happen with Pete, and yet here she was, letting it happen with Dax. Not following her own instincts, not letting her own feelings for him be the deciding factor.

Because as she sat on her daughter's bed, still staring at Dax's photograph, there was no denying that her feelings for him were nothing to sneeze at. They were no less than the feelings she'd had for Pete. And if her feelings for Pete had been big enough, strong enough not to bend to the potential of a life-threatening disease, weren't her feelings now big and strong enough not to bend to the shadow of Dax's past or his reputation?

She thought that they were.

And if they were, they were also big and strong and important enough to take a risk for.

Shandie let that realization settle in, waiting to see if it would stick or if, in another moment, some other thought might shoo it away.

But no other thoughts, no other feelings could unseat it. This *was* the real thing, she decided.

In fact, the only other thought that popped into her head was that there were a few indications that Dax *did* have some staying power. He'd stayed in his hometown, hadn't he? He'd maintained his friendships with his childhood friends. If he could do that, maybe he had the ability to go the distance with her and Kayla, too. Maybe his poor track record with Allaire and Lizbeth did have more to do with the times of his life and the situations themselves—the way he'd claimed.

So, just as the possibility that Pete's cancer might have never returned, there was, at the very least, the possibility that she and Dax and Kayla could have a full future together....

"Just don't let me be wrong," she beseeched his image.

And now that she'd made up her mind to take that chance on him that he'd asked her to take, she wanted to put the wheels into motion. She wanted to see him. To tell him. To end this misery she'd put them all through.

And returning her daughter's ill-gotten gains seemed like the perfect excuse.

Shandie stood, taking the framed photograph with her and went into her own room.

She was in too much of a hurry to get to Dax to waste time changing out of the jeans and buttoned-up cardigan sweater she had on. But she did powder her nose and under her eyes to conceal the redness left by her tears.

She also refreshed her blush and mascara, and applied a little lip gloss.

Then she took her hair down from the clip that held it haphazardly at the back of her head and brushed the golden strands to fall around her face.

"Ready or not, here I come," she whispered to her reflection, turning off the loud television as she went by it on her way out with the stolen goods in hand.

She snatched her coat off the hall tree when she reached the entry, deciding that rather than driving up the street to Dax's place, she'd walk and put her coat on along the way.

Then she opened her front door and stopped short.

Because there, standing on the other side of the threshold, was Dax, leaning on one arm stretched up the door frame as if he'd been there quite a while.

Which was given credence when he said, "Finally."

"Finally?" Shandie parroted, surprised to find him on her porch and confused by his greeting.

"I've been out here ringing the bell and pounding on the door for ten minutes."

"I had the television on loud."

"I know, I could hear it."

He didn't wait for an invitation inside or even ask if he could come in. He merely pushed off the jamb and came, leaving Shandie no option but to step out of his way.

She did that, rehanging her coat on the hall tree.

When she turned to face him again, he was right there, standing directly in front of her.

Without taking his eyes off her, he shoved the door closed behind him. "We're gonna talk," he decreed. "I know Kayla's gone to her sleepover so we can scream and holler and throw things if we need to, but *we are going to talk,*" he added, those last five words drawn out and emphasized.

"I was on my way to see you," Shandie said.

"Yeah?"

She handed him the framed photograph. "Kayla must have taken this. It was hidden under her pillow."

Dax took it, glanced at it, shook his head and chuckled a little wryly. "She must have swiped it off the wall when I wasn't looking."

He set the picture on the side table where Shandie usually put her mail when she first came in, but he did that without moving from his position facing her.

"Kayla can have it," he said of the photograph, his gaze still on it. "She can have anything she wants from me."

Then he looked back at Shandie. "Is that the only reason you were coming to see me? To return it?"

"No," Shandie admitted freely because four days was too much time to have wasted already. "I wanted to talk, too."

"It better be about how this whole split between us isn't going to go on," he warned. "Because if you just want to talk about keeping Kayla away from the shop, forget about it. I'm not letting you do this, Shandie. I'm in love with you. I love Kayla. Unless I'm mistaken, Kayla loves me. And so do you—"

"I do," Shandie confirmed, cutting him off and surprising him. "I do love you. *That's* what I was coming to see you about. To tell you I love you as much as I loved Pete."

One side of his mouth lifted in a cocky half smile, and he took a step nearer to her. "Is that so?"

"Yes, that's so," she said, going on to explain all she'd been thinking about and laying out for him the decisions she'd ultimately arrived at. "So I'm betting on you having more staying power with me than you had with Allaire or Lizbeth Stanton," she concluded.

"Oh, I have staying power," he assured her when she'd finished, putting a much more sensual spin on it than she had as he slid his hands from her wrists to her upper arms and pulled her nearer. "You're never getting rid of me."

"I hope not," she said more quietly.

"You don't have to hope, Shandie," he assured, serious himself once more. "That's why I came here tonight—to fight this out, to see it through, to let you know that I was going to do anything and everything it took to convince you that no matter what my history is and no matter how fast this has happened between us, I'm in. I'm in to my eyeballs and I don't want out. Not even if you'd have made it tough on me tonight. I may not have known the real thing from the not real thing before, but now? Now I know the real thing because I have some experience with the not real thing to compare it to. And the real thing is so damn much better, so damn much more powerful, so damn much more all-consuming, that what I've felt before can't hold a candle to it. And I'm sure as hell not letting it go.

I'm not letting you go. I'm not letting Kayla go. Not ever."

"It's a deal," she said as if they'd been bargaining with each other.

"That's it?" he asked with that cocky grin again.

"That's it."

He studied her face for a long moment, a shade of disbelief edging his expression. Then he said, "You'll marry me? Let me be a dad to Kayla?"

"That's the plan."

He grinned a full, delighted grin. "You had a plan?"

Shandie grinned back at him. "No, it just sounded good."

He laughed and pulled her into his arms to kiss her then, a kiss that began sweetly and almost instantly turned into something riddled with passion.

Then he stopped kissing her, pointed his chin in the direction of the stairs behind her and said, "Kayla's really gone, huh?"

"For the whole night."

"I think I better put my money where my mouth is and prove my staying power, then," he said, bending over to wrap his arms just under her rump to lift her over his shoulder like a sack of grain.

"This is not romantic," she informed him from upside down as he carried her up the stairs, taking two at a time.

But all he said was, "Which room?" when he reached the second floor.

"First door on the left," Shandie answered with a laugh.

He took her into her room, not bothering to turn on the light, and deposited her unceremoniously on her double bed. Then, with his eyes holding steady on hers, he ripped off his denim jacket, peeled his T-shirt over his head and climbed onto the bed with his jeans-clad legs straddling her while his mouth recaptured hers.

Shandie didn't mind that from there his kiss was hungry and demanding because she felt the same hunger, the same demands. She didn't even hesitate to hook her fingers into the waistband of his jeans and unfasten them before using the open ends to yank him down on top of her.

A part of her marveled at where they were, what they were doing, how quickly it had evolved into this, but another part of her merely indulged in meeting the needs she hadn't even known she'd been fostering as hands coursed under clothing to remove it and then trailed across bare skin. As mouths and tongues toyed with each other and then did some exploring of different frontiers. As they rolled around together and discovered new ways to please, to pleasure, to arouse and drive wild until Dax slipped inside of her and truly proved his theory that they were two halves of a whole made perfect when they were joined together.

So perfect that even once they'd both reached the pinnacle of that pleasure that they each brought the other to, he stayed joined with her, holding her so close she wasn't sure where he ended and she began as he rolled them to lie on their sides.

"I love you, Shandie," he whispered into her hair. "I love you like I have never loved anyone."

"I love you, too, Dax. With all my heart."

With all her soul. With every breath she took.

"And we can be a family?" he asked with so much awe for that idea in his voice it brought tears to her eyes.

"A family for the holidays," she said.

"And for the rest of time, too."

"I guess so if I'm never getting rid of you," she teased him.

He flexed inside of her. "Never."

Then she heard him take a deep breath and sigh it out before he relaxed around her, still holding her firmly against him, his arms encircling her, one thick leg draped over her thigh.

Shandie closed her eyes and imagined how thrilled her daughter would be when she told Kayla that Dax was going to be a part of their lives after all.

Her daughter, who had brought them all together.

Twice, actually—that first day when Kayla had gone to buy a "big bike" from Dax, and again today when the little girl had just wanted to be with him.

Which was what Shandie wanted, too— just to be with him.

That was something she'd wondered if she would ever find again after Pete, but she was glad she had.

And somehow at that moment, lying there with Dax, she felt as if he was a gift that maybe Pete had sent to her and Kayla.

An early Christmas gift that gave Kayla someone who Shandie had no doubt already did love her daughter and care about her and want only what was best for the little girl.

A gift that gave Shandie someone to share the rest of her life with.

Which she suddenly felt sure was exactly how long she and Dax would have together.

* * * * *

YES! Please send me **The Montana Mavericks Collection** in Larger Print. This collection begins with 3 FREE books and 2 FREE gifts (gifts valued at approx. $20.00 retail) in the first shipment, along with the other first 4 books from the collection! If I do not cancel, I will receive 8 monthly shipments until I have the entire 51-book Montana Mavericks collection. I will receive 2 or 3 FREE books in each shipment and I will pay just $4.99 US/ $5.89 CDN for each of the other four books in each shipment, plus $2.99 for shipping and handling per shipment.*If I decide to keep the entire collection, I'll have paid for only 32 books, because 19 books are FREE! I understand that accepting the 3 free books and gifts places me under no obligation to buy anything. I can always return a shipment and cancel at any time. My free books and gifts are mine to keep no matter what I decide.

263 HCN 2404   463 HCN 2404

Name	(PLEASE PRINT)	
Address		Apt. #
City	State/Prov.	Zip/Postal Code

Signature (if under 18, a parent or guardian must sign)

Mail to the **Reader Service:**
IN U.S.A.: P.O. Box 1867, Buffalo, NY 14240-1867
IN CANADA: P.O. Box 609, Fort Erie, Ontario L2A 5X3

* Terms and prices subject to change without notice. Prices do not include applicable taxes. Sales tax applicable in N.Y. Canadian residents will be charged applicable taxes. This offer is limited to one order per household. All orders subject to approval. Credit or debit balances in a customer's account(s) may be offset by any other outstanding balance owed by or to the customer. Please allow 4 to 6 weeks for delivery. Offer available while quantities last. Offer not available to Quebec residents.

Your Privacy—The Reader Service is committed to protecting your privacy. Our Privacy Policy is available online at www.ReaderService.com or upon request from the Reader Service.

We make a portion of our mailing list available to reputable third parties that offer products we believe may interest you. If you prefer that we not exchange your name with third parties, or if you wish to clarify or modify your communication preferences, please visit us at www.ReaderService.com/consumerschoice or write to us at Reader Service Preference Service, P.O. Box 9062, Buffalo, NY 14269. Include your complete name and address.

REQUEST YOUR FREE BOOKS!
2 FREE NOVELS PLUS 2 FREE GIFTS!

H HARLEQUIN®

SPECIAL EDITION
Life, Love & Family

YES! Please send me 2 FREE Harlequin® Special Edition novels and my 2 FREE gifts (gifts are worth about $10). After receiving them, if I don't wish to receive any more books, I can return the shipping statement marked "cancel." If I don't cancel, I will receive 6 brand-new novels every month and be billed just $4.74 per book in the U.S. or $5.24 per book in Canada. That's a savings of at least 14% off the cover price! It's quite a bargain! Shipping and handling is just 50¢ per book in the U.S. and 75¢ per book in Canada.* I understand that accepting the 2 free books and gifts places me under no obligation to buy anything. I can always return a shipment and cancel at any time. Even if I never buy another book, the two free books and gifts are mine to keep forever.

235/335 HDN F46C

Name	(PLEASE PRINT)	
Address		Apt. #
City	State/Prov.	Zip/Postal Code

Signature (if under 18, a parent or guardian must sign)

Mail to the **Harlequin® Reader Service:**
IN U.S.A.: P.O. Box 1867, Buffalo, NY 14240-1867
IN CANADA: P.O. Box 609, Fort Erie, Ontario L2A 5X3

Want to try two free books from another line?
Call 1-800-873-8635 or visit www.ReaderService.com.

* Terms and prices subject to change without notice. Prices do not include applicable taxes. Sales tax applicable in N.Y. Canadian residents will be charged applicable taxes. Offer not valid in Quebec. This offer is limited to one order per household. Not valid for current subscribers to Harlequin Special Edition books. All orders subject to credit approval. Credit or debit balances in a customer's account(s) may be offset by any other outstanding balance owed by or to the customer. Please allow 4 to 6 weeks for delivery. Offer available while quantities last.

Your Privacy—The Harlequin® Reader Service is committed to protecting your privacy. Our Privacy Policy is available online at www.ReaderService.com or upon request from the Harlequin Reader Service.

We make a portion of our mailing list available to reputable third parties that offer products we believe may interest you. If you prefer that we not exchange your name with third parties, or if you wish to clarify or modify your communication preferences, please visit us at www.ReaderService.com/consumerchoice or write to us at Harlequin Reader Service Preference Service, P.O. Box 9062, Buffalo, NY 14269. Include your complete name and address.

HSEDIR13R

REQUEST YOUR FREE BOOKS!
2 FREE NOVELS PLUS 2 FREE GIFTS!

 HARLEQUIN®

 American ★ Romance®

LOVE, HOME & HAPPINESS

YES! Please send me 2 FREE Harlequin® American Romance® novels and my 2 FREE gifts (gifts are worth about $10). After receiving them, if I don't wish to receive any more books, I can return the shipping statement marked "cancel." If I don't cancel, I will receive 4 brand-new novels every month and be billed just $4.74 per book in the U.S. or $5.24 per book in Canada. That's a savings of at least 14% off the cover price! It's quite a bargain! Shipping and handling is just 50¢ per book in the U.S. and 75¢ per book in Canada.* I understand that accepting the 2 free books and gifts places me under no obligation to buy anything. I can always return a shipment and cancel at any time. Even if I never buy another book, the two free books and gifts are mine to keep forever.

154/354 HDN F4YY

Name _____ (PLEASE PRINT) _____

Address _____ Apt. # _____

City _____ State/Prov. _____ Zip/Postal Code _____

Signature (if under 18, a parent or guardian must sign) _____

Mail to the Harlequin® Reader Service:
IN U.S.A.: P.O. Box 1867, Buffalo, NY 14240-1867
IN CANADA: P.O. Box 609, Fort Erie, Ontario L2A 5X3

Want to try two free books from another line?
Call 1-800-873-8635 or visit www.ReaderService.com.

* Terms and prices subject to change without notice. Prices do not include applicable taxes. Sales tax applicable in N.Y. Canadian residents will be charged applicable taxes. Offer not valid in Quebec. This offer is limited to one order per household. Not valid for current subscribers to Harlequin American Romance books. All orders subject to credit approval. Credit or debit balances in a customer's account(s) may be offset by any other outstanding balance owed by or to the customer. Please allow 4 to 6 weeks for delivery. Offer available while quantities last.

Your Privacy—The Harlequin® Reader Service is committed to protecting your privacy. Our Privacy Policy is available online at www.ReaderService.com or upon request from the Harlequin Reader Service.

We make a portion of our mailing list available to reputable third parties that offer products we believe may interest you. If you prefer that we not exchange your name with third parties, or if you wish to clarify or modify your communication preferences, please visit us at www.ReaderService.com/consumerschoice or write to us at Harlequin Reader Service Preference Service, P.O. Box 9062, Buffalo, NY 14269. Include your complete name and address.

HARDIR13R